NOT YOUR AVERAGE GIRL

JOANNE RYAN

Other Books By Joanne Ryan
The Lodger
Without Reason
The Double
All The Lost Years
One Night
Lie To Me

Writing as Marina Johnson
Fat Girl Slim
Fat Girl Slim Returns
Fat Girl Slim Three
A Confusion of Murders
Say Hello & Wave Goodbye
So Talk To Me
The Harriet Way
The Herb Sisters

CHAPTER ONE

Near the end of the course today, Rachel asked us to think of three words to describe ourselves and to write them down. She's got a bit carried away with herself these past three days and is forgetting that she's just an admin clerk teaching the long-term unemployed how to apply for a job. If any of us even get a job we're going to end up working in a supermarket or a fast-food outlet so I don't know why she's bothering.

Rachel is enthusiastic and jolly; she says she wants to help us make something of ourselves, whatever that means. She tries to ignore the fact that we're only here because our benefits will stop if we don't attend.

Since I have to write something I thought why not tell it like it is because no one else is going to see what I write. Carla and Roxy on the desk in front of me keep giggling and nudging each other every time they turn and look at me and I can't help but overhear what they say. It's not even overhearing, actually, because they want me to hear. *Ugly fat cow* and *retard* feature frequently in their loud whisperings; not very original and trust me, I've heard far worse. And I'm actually not fat at all but maybe I look a bit chunky in my big, baggy t-shirt. I'm not a retard either but I can see why they might think that I am. When they giggle and do their loud whispering Rachel looks over at them with a frown from her desk at the front of the room but she doesn't tell them off. I can't blame her; they're a couple of bitches and she wouldn't want to get on the wrong side of them even though Rachel is supposed to be the one in charge. Anyway, it's not as if we're at school and she has any real power; and even if she was brave enough to tell them off they'd just give her a mouthful.

I never stand up to them or say anything when they call me names because they would be much nastier to me if I did. If I've learned anything, it's that it's best to keep a low profile and keep my mouth shut and eventually people will get bored and move onto someone else.

The other seven people in this room are just relieved that it's not them that they're picking on so no one is challenging Carla and Roxy for their behaviour, either. They all ignore me as well because they don't want it to look as if they're on my side in case they get picked on too. Luckily this is the last day of the course and I'll never have to see or hear any of them ever again after today. I'm so used to insults that they don't bother me anymore; words can't hurt me and are far preferable to physical violence. I regret that thought as soon as it pops into my head and quickly push it away because it conjures up a vision of Aaron's huge, meaty fist steaming towards me.

I concentrate and stare down at the sheet of paper.

Three words to describe myself.

I'm probably supposed to put something like hard-working or helpful but I'll be honest, because honesty is much more interesting that lying. Besides which, no one is going to see what I've written because it's for my eyes only; this is a *cheat sheet* to add to the pack of papers which is supposed to help me improve my chance of actually being offered employment when I start applying for jobs.

It'll go straight into the bin when I get home.

I could put *victim.* Mimi said I was always playing the victim but I prefer to use another word that means victim but sounds *sort* of useful, as if I'm actually doing something for someone.

DOORMAT, I write.

I let people walk all over me and wipe their feet on me over and over again and I never complain. And while it may not be doing me any good, it's making someone else feel better. I've been like this since the day I was born; not that I can remember the day I was born but I've been like it for as long as I can remember. I was the kid standing on her own in the corner of the playground who none of the other kids wanted to play with. The only time anyone used to bother with me was when they were a bit bored and fed up with playing *tig* or *what's the time Mr Wolf* and they fancied a change. I always knew when it was coming because a crowd would gather and the one with the biggest mouth would step forward. They would say that they liked my dress or something equally untrue and then the crowd would collapse into laughter. This was followed by one of them shouting that I smelled and more hoots of laughter would follow. Maybe I did smell, I think it's probable that I did. I was a child; what do children know about washing? I never used to answer back then, either.

LAZY. I write next. Aaron used to tell me I was a *lazy fat cow* or a *lazy bitch* at least ten times a day so I'll put that. I don't think I am lazy but even if I was there's nothing wrong with being lazy because it's not hurting anyone else, is it? Aaron said the flat was a tip and that I was too lazy to look after it but he was the one that made all the mess and he never cleared up, so why should I? I always kept it neat and tidy before he arrived but once he was there it was a permanent pigsty.

Aaron was nice to me at first but it didn't last long; about as long as it took for me to agree to let him move into my flat, actually. Niceness never lasts and from my experience it just means that someone wants something from you. Although

Mimi was never nice to me to get what she wanted, she just took it. She was lazy too; she used to sit around smoking cigarettes and eating all day but to hear her talk you'd think she didn't sit down from the moment she got up in the morning until she went to bed at night.

I chew the end of my pen as I consider what I'm going to write for the third and final word and then stop mid-chew and lay the pen down on the desk. It's dawned on me that someone else has used the pen before me and most likely chewed the end of it, too.

Okay, one more word and I'm done and then maybe if everyone else has done their three words, too, Rachel will let us finish early because surely three days is long enough to learn how to apply for a shit job that none of us actually want.

I think hard, even though none of this matters, and try my best to find the *exact* word that will describe me, because I don't think *doormat* and *lazy*, do me justice.

Inspiration strikes and I smile to myself as I pick up the pen and pull the sheet of paper towards me. I begin to write in neat capital letters.

MURDERER.

CHAPTER TWO

I was nine-years-old before I realised that Mimi was a foster carer. The kids at school told me; they said that my real mum didn't want me because I was fat and ugly and that Mimi only looked after me because she was being paid and making pots of money out of me. I had no idea how they knew this and I didn't; it was only as I got older that I realised that one of them must have overheard their mother or a teacher talking about me.

I didn't believe them – I didn't *want* to believe them – and when I got home from school I told Mimi what they'd said and she laughed loudly, but not in a funny way. She said what she was being paid by the social barely covered my food and clothing and that she was looking after me out of the goodness of her heart. I never mentioned it again after that because she had that look on her face when I told her; the look that says *don't push it or you'll be sorry*. I didn't want to get on the wrong side of her because if I did, even though it meant I would get a week off school until the bruises had faded, I didn't want to take the chance that this time she might actually kill me. Her punishments were few and far between now; mostly because I'd learned how to avoid triggering them, but the violence had become more intense; as if because she'd saved it up, she had more to give.

So even though I didn't dare ask her, I badly wanted to know how much money she was being paid. I don't know why I wanted to know; I just did. All of my clothes came from charity shops and jumble sales and she used to moan if she paid more than a pound for anything so I had a suspicion that she was lying. I used to believe everything she said when I was little but by then I'd started to have my suspicions about her and I was beginning to realise that most families weren't like ours. Our meals mainly consisted of chips from the chippy with some bread and margarine if there was any in the larder. Mimi always had a pie or piece of fish with her chips but I never did. She said I wouldn't like it so there was no point in wasting the money on me. Breakfast was bread and margarine if I was really lucky but mostly I went to school on an empty stomach. I got school dinners and was always the first in the queue for seconds but I know for a fact that they were free because the teacher never asked me for my dinner money like she did with the other kids. And even if I hadn't noticed that I didn't have to pay, the other kids did.

So after the *carer* conversation, I went upstairs to my bedroom and sat on my bed and thought back over the last week. Then I wrote down the cost of the chips in the back of my school maths book and added it all up. I didn't add in the bread and marge because I knew they wouldn't make much difference. I knew exactly how much the chips were though because she always used to send me to the chippy to buy them.

I can remember even now that the total didn't reach double figures.

It was a shock when I found out about her being a foster carer because I honestly thought that she was my auntie until then. She'd always made me call her Aunt Mimi and she was the only person that I could remember living with. I never knew what happened to my real parents because Mimi never told me and I never asked. I reasoned that they didn't want me so what else was there to know?

With hindsight, I should have guessed about Mimi being a foster carer, because every few months a lady with a briefcase would turn up at the door. Mimi would have made a bit of an effort for her visit and put on a dress and washed her hair and she'd put on this posh sort of talking that sounded a bit like the queen on a bad day. Mimi and the lady would go into the lounge together and close the door while I hovered in the hallway outside listening to the low murmur of their voices. I could never hear what they said no matter how hard I tried, which was amazing as Mimi usually had the loudest voice and the biggest mouth.

After they'd been in there talking for a while, Mimi would open the lounge door and I'd be summoned in to join them. The lady would ask me questions like how was I feeling and if I was enjoying school and I'd answer with the replies that Mimi had told me to say. The lady would nod and smile and then I knew that I'd said the right things and that Mimi would be fine with me once the lady had gone. When the lady had left, the new clothes that Mimi had bought for me to wear for the visit would go back to the shop for a refund and life would carry on as normal.

Except than one day the lady turned up unannounced; that was the first time that I ever saw Mimi afraid although at the time I didn't understand why. I was ten-years-old and I stood there and said nothing while Mimi told her that I was going through a *difficult patch* and that she didn't know what to do with me. She told her that I was refusing to wash or wear any of the new clothes that she'd bought for me and insisted on wearing old, scruffy clothes that were too small for me. She said that she was about to ring the lady herself to ask for help if she hadn't just turned up.

Looking back I think that the school must have contacted social services because I looked so neglected but I didn't know that at the time. Mimi didn't do much in the way of washing clothes because she wasn't bothered about stuff like that; she said too much water washed the guts out of clothes. She didn't make me wash either, which suited me fine because washing was boring. That was one of the reasons why I didn't have any friends and the other kids called me *smelly Ellie*.

The lady wasn't as smiley as usual on that visit and she told me that I had to do as Mimi said because it was for my own good otherwise they would have to put *special measures* in place. I had no idea what *special measures* were but to my ten-year-old ears they sounded painful and I had a vision of a metal ruler for some reason. I agreed that I would do whatever Mimi said even though I always did anyway.

After the lady had gone I was expecting some sort of punishment but Mimi surprised me and kept her hands off me. She said that if the child catcher came for me and put me in the children's prison it would all be my own fault for being so lazy. She said that she didn't have time to do everything for me when I should be doing it for myself so if I wanted to stay living with her I'd better buck my ideas up.

I wasn't sure if the child catcher was real or not but I wasn't taking any chances so I learned how to use the washing machine and I started to look after myself. I began washing and cleaning my teeth and wearing clean clothes instead of the same thing for weeks on end. And Mimi quite liked it because then I could wash *her* clothes for her, too, which gave her more time to sit and watch her programmes on TV. Not that she wanted them washed very often.

So I didn't look so neglected anymore and we had no more surprise visits from social services and I didn't see that scared look on Mimi's face again for a very long time. I still got called *smelly Ellie* at school although I didn't smell anymore, because once you've got a nickname, it sticks forever. That name followed me until I left school at sixteen and it only stopped then because once I'd left I made sure that I didn't see anyone from school ever again.

'Do you want to come in, Ellen?'

Fred the fryer's words interrupt my reminiscing. He's holding the door open that goes into the back of the chip shop and beckoning me to go through to the back kitchen. I've been made to apply for this job and he's interviewing me for the position of kitchen assistant. While I've been sitting here waiting on one of the rickety chairs that are provided for customers while they wait for their order, I've been remembering my life with Mimi and my frequent trips here. I've spent a good portion of my life in this chippy and although I don't visit quite as much as I used to, I'm still a regular customer.

I stand up and follow Fred through to the back kitchen and wonder why we're bothering with this charade; we both know that I'm going to get the job because applicants aren't exactly lining up outside the door. Working in a chippy is hardly a career choice, is it? I put all thoughts of Mimi aside as I follow him because she's in my past now. I don't even know why I was dragging it all up in my head again.

She's gone now, so what's the point of looking back?

I hope Fred doesn't ask me about her because I don't want to have to explain.

Maybe he won't; maybe he already knows that she's dead.

I got the job, obviously, and I start tomorrow. I could have started tonight but I told Fred that I couldn't as I had to go out. A complete lie but I really couldn't be bothered and Coronation Street is on tonight, anyway. Luckily, he didn't ask me about Mimi so I didn't have to go through the whole boring story again. Maybe he already knows or perhaps he's forgotten I lived with her; she only ever came to the chippy when she wanted to put a bet on at the bookies next door. The betting thing was a recent fad with her and she tried to make me do it for her but I deliberately messed it up so she'd have to do it herself. I hated going in there and seeing all the sad men with their desperate faces as they watched the races on the telly.

I really don't want the job and I'm pissed off that I've been forced into it. I was quite content living on benefits but thanks to Rachel and that 'course' I've been press-ganged into it. I don't know why they can't just leave me alone because it's not as if I cost the state very much; a tiny council flat that has damp and really needs demolishing and weekly benefits that are barely enough to live on for most people. Some people cost far more than me, what about those huge fat people that have to have carers looking after them and can't work? They don't make them get a job, do they? No they don't; they employ people to get food for them so they can get even fatter and carers to wash them because they're too fat to do it themselves. I've seen the TV programmes so I know what I'm talking about.

I don't have expensive tastes; I don't smoke or drink or bother with fashionable clothes so I can live quite comfortably on my benefits now that Aaron has gone. I have my plans and in the not too distant future I'll be saying goodbye to this place forever but for now, I'll carry on as usual.

Mimi.

She keeps popping up even though she's been gone for nearly a year. I just can't seem to get rid of her from my thoughts. I suppose it'll take time for her to go completely because she was pretty much my whole life for such a long time. It seems odd to me that when she was alive no-one bothered nagging at me to get a job but as soon as she'd gone the social haven't left me alone. Absolute pestering. It's a shame they didn't take a bit more notice of me when I was a kid and she was my foster carer and then maybe I'd have had a fighting chance at a decent life.

I put thoughts of Mimi aside and concentrate on my new employment. I suppose I'll have to turn up and actually do the job for a while to show willing to prevent my benefits from being terminated. I don't want to draw any attention to myself so I'll have to go along with it. I'll be barely any better off but at least I'll get free chips for a while. I don't intend staying and I'll make sure that Fred gets fed up with me pretty quickly and has to *let me go.* A couple of weeks should do it. I'll mess up people's orders and get the change wrong which will lose him money and he won't be able to get rid of me fast enough.

I can play the thicko extremely well because I've been playing it for most of my life and people expect it from me. It helps that my GCSE's are the lowest grades possible – not that Fred asked – pretty much all that was required to pass them was to write my name at the top of the page and make a pathetic attempt at a few questions. It was laughable, really. The teachers at my secondary school treated me as if I was almost subnormal – if they noticed me at all. I was doing quite well in primary school to begin with but I soon discovered that being a social outcast because of Mimi's neglect was made ten times worse by also being the class swot; kids, in particular, don't like a clever clogs.

If you're going to be the butt of everyone's jokes you have to be less than them, not more. I went from a keen student who wanted to learn everything to the dullard who had to be told how to do something twenty times and yet still managed to fuck it up. The teachers soon gave up on me; there were a few keen ones but even they stopped bothering with me after a while because they just don't have the time to waste on someone who won't or can't learn. Plus, I kept getting head lice and no teacher wants to give one-to-one learning to a kid with nits.

Perhaps I could have used my brains to change my life because I *am* clever, I have no doubt about that. I could easily have outwitted and exceeded most of my fellow classmates had I chosen to but I knew that it was pointless. I was never going to go to university or have a career because Mimi would never allow it. She'd been telling me for as long as I could remember that because she'd looked after me, I would be repaying her by looking after her when she was old. So I knew that trying to achieve anything would be a waste of time. When I left school my life barely changed, except that Mimi got fatter and I started buying my own clothes from the market out of my benefits. If only I'd realised sooner that the older I got, the less power Mimi had over me. The trouble was, she'd controlled me for so long that I thought there was no way out.

There's always a way out.

It's not too late to get educated and get a career, I suppose, because I'm only twenty-one and Mimi's no longer a problem.

But I don't want to get educated.

Because when people assume that you're stupid, it's very useful.

CHAPTER THREE

I leave the flat for the ten minute walk to the chippy to work my first shift. The sun is shining and the air is very hot even though it's nearly five o'clock. I pass a few fellow benefit-ites like myself – I know this because they are regulars at the social – and most of them are dressed in t-shirts and shorts or skimpy little cotton dresses that barely cover their arses. Perfectly suitable for an unusually hot, July day but I continue to wear what I always wear, summer or winter, except that in the summer I don't put my coat on unless it's really cold. A long, baggy, over-sized, beige t-shirt over black leggings finished off with black trainers. My only concession to summer is that the leggings are mid-calf length instead of to the ankle and I don't wear socks so my glaringly white legs are on display.

I have very pale skin as I never sunbathe; I have nowhere *to* sunbathe as I live in a third floor flat. Besides which, I prefer to stay pale as the sun would bring out the smattering of freckles on my face and make my nose turn red. My hair is not quite ginger but more of a strawberry blonde. I think that it's a pretty colour but for some reason, other people don't and they refer to me as a 'ginger', with a hard 'g'. I also have pretty good teeth considering that I never started cleaning them until I was ten but no one ever sees them as I rarely smile.

Unlike me, the other tower block residents never let the fact that they don't have a garden stop them from sun bathing. Groups of them habitually congregate on the patchy grass in front of the flats when the weather is warm. They doss around drinking cheap cider from cans and smoking cigarettes and the men take their shirts off and some of the women take their tops off and sunbathe in their grubby bras. The hotter the weather, the more of them there are and one of them usually has some sort of radio or an iPhone blasting out loud music.

I hate it when the weather's good because I have to walk past them and it's like being back at school with the sniggering and fake wolf whistles and hoots of derision. Why can't people just shut up and mind their own business? I don't understand why I'm so interesting to others when there's piss-taking to be done because the rest of the time I'm invisible. I don't even stand out; I make sure to dress in the blandest clothes possible but I still seem to be the target for other people's nastiness.

I'm not fat, not thin, and I'm not ugly. I'm nondescript and ignored until boredom sets in and people start looking around to see who they can pick on.

The general opinion is that you should stand up to bullies but I've found in my experience that this doesn't work unless it's on a one to one basis. Most of the bullies – aside from Mimi and Aaron – have come in packs and I can't stand up to a big bunch of them, can I, because I'm just going to get my head kicked in. I couldn't stand up to Mimi or Aaron either and there was only one of them so whoever said you should stand up to bullies has obviously never been bullied. Or perhaps they were a bully themselves but they didn't realise it. Who knows. So I do what I've always done when the cat-calling starts; I put my head down and carry on walking as if I can't hear them.

But it never gets any easier.

Thankfully, today, I escape the laughs and comments as the combination of sun and cheap cider has dulled their already dull senses and most of them appear to be asleep or in a drunken stupor.

I've made no special preparations for my first shift; my hair is tied up in its usual ponytail and I'm assuming that I'll be given some sort of overall to wear as I don't have one of my own. I'm going to smell like a chip shop by the time I've finished work and even though my shift doesn't finish until half-past-ten I'm going to have to shower and wash my hair when I get home. Most normal people would be feeling a bit nervous and excited if they'd never had a job before and they were starting their very first one at the age of twenty-one, but I'm not.

Because I'm not normal.

Okay, maybe I'm a bit nervous but I'm definitely not excited. I wish I was normal but it's a fact that I'm not; it's not my fault but no one else seems to realise that I didn't ask to be like this. Do people think that I *want* to be a social outcast? Of course I don't – I want what everyone else wants; friends, a love life and a family, but I have none of those things. Never have done and never will. No one *wants* to be the person that everyone else thinks is stupid and is only here to be used as the butt of pathetic jokes that make the rest of the world feel superior. For some unknown reason, life has singled me out to be the outcast and I can't do a thing about it. Hash tags like *be kind* may be bandied around willy-nilly but in real life, very few people are kind or if they are, they're not kind to me.

I thought that my life had changed when I met Aaron because he treated me nicely for a while. I bumped into him at the bus stop when I was waiting to catch the bus to go and sign on. I was surprised when he started talking to me because men never bother with me, not even the ugly, stupid ones who aren't fussy and will shag anything that moves. And Aaron wasn't ugly, he was *fit*. Not film star fit but he had his own teeth, a full head of hair and he wasn't fat, which around here is pretty outstanding for a thirty-year-old man. This is a rough estate and most of the men here have at least the beginnings of a beer belly and one missing tooth by thirty – either because it's been knocked out or because they've never owned a toothbrush.

Aaron was nice and he was easy to talk to and the attention felt pretty amazing to start with. He seemed like a man of the world because he was a lot older than me, too, although as I got to know him I realised that he was actually pretty dim. I couldn't understand for the life of me why he was interested in me and I told him this right from the off. He said it was because I was different and not like the rest of the slags that live around here.

Stupidly, I fell for it; me, who thinks she's so clever. Of course, he was only being nice to me because he wanted something. As soon as he got what he wanted – my flat – he treated me like shit, the same as everyone else does. He said I was a retard and should be grateful that he even wanted to be in the same room as me, let alone live with me. He used to say he was doing me a favour shagging me because let's face it, men were hardly beating down the door to get to me.

The bastard; to think that I gave up my virginity for him.

That was when I realised that no matter what people say, I can't trust anyone but myself and as long as I remember that I'll be fine. Aaron thought that he had a God given right to take over my flat and treat me like a slave. I was supposed to shut up and do as he said and be pathetically grateful for any morsel of attention that he threw my way.

Anyway, he's gone now and I have the flat to myself again and no one is ever moving in again. Although maybe I'm being too hard on myself because I wasn't completely taken in by him. I never did trust him enough to tell him Mimi's secret.

Or mine.

I've arrived. The scruffy row of shops looms up in front of me and I walk around to the back alleyway to the rear entrances of the shops. Fred the fryer is standing by the open back door of the chippy smoking a roll up. He frowns when he sees me and I can see him mentally wondering who the hell I am. I'm used to it; being instantly forgettable and yet instantly noticeable when an object of ridicule is required.

'Ellie,' I say, to spare him the mental machinations. 'I start today.'

'Oh, yeah, course,' he says, flicking the wet, mashed end of his cigarette expertly towards a huge pile of rubbish in the corner. 'Follow me.'

I watch as Fred rummages around in a cardboard box on the floor and pulls out a blue nylon overall which he holds out towards me with a grunt when he finally manages to stand upright. I think the effort of bending over with his huge stomach in the way has taken it out of him. I take the overall from him and find that even holding it in my hands is unpleasant; I can smell the chip fat emanating from it and it feels greasy to the touch. I'm pretty certain that someone else has worn it before me and that it hasn't been washed. I don't consider myself an overly fussy person and I may wear the same clothes everyday but they are always clean. My clothes may *look* exactly the same – and they are, because I buy the same items several times over – but they're fresh on every day. Mimi's neglect when I was a child has ensured that since I've been old enough to fend for myself I cannot bear to wear dirty clothes or to be dirty. I can live very frugally but I cannot skimp on washing powder or shower gel; I just can't do it. I no longer need to be frugal but it's become such a habit that I can't seem to shake it off.

I stare down at the overall and wonder what I'm going to do; I have a real fear of putting it on over my clean clothes but I'm not going to refuse, am I? Because that would involve confrontation and I don't do confrontation and also, if I refuse to wear it I won't be able to do even one shift and the social might stop my benefits.

'Put it on then, love, 'cos we're opening in ten minutes.' Fred is staring at me with his arms stretched across his huge stomach and he's frowning. He's not wearing an overall but has a once-white, now grey, massive cotton apron stretched around his middle. It looks like he's been wearing it for years and has never washed it. The dirt has given it an almost leather-like appearance and for the first time I notice his fingernails. I feel myself about to gag. His nails are long with black dirt ingrained underneath them; to think that I ate from this chip shop for years and never noticed how filthy he is. He coughs and I can hear the phlegm rattle in his throat. Eager to get away from him in case I puke, I slip my arms into the overall and pull it around me and do up the buttons on the front. I'll have to wear it but it'll be going straight into the washing machine on a very hot wash when I get home tonight.

Fred has already told me that there will only be two of us working behind the counter tonight as the third assistant is off sick. I'm hoping that the person I'm working with will be someone old. I find that generally, older people are more accepting of me and less likely to make me the butt of their jokes. Not always, but usually. Whoever it is, I won't be working here for very long, a week at the most I should think, because as soon as I start messing everything up Fred will want rid of me. So even if my co-worker is okay with me to start with they won't be when I start making mistakes and making their life more difficult with my thickness. I'm not looking forward to it and for the millionth time I curse Rachel and that stupid course.

'I'll introduce you to Tash and she'll show you

the ropes.' Fred is staring at me and I realise I've been daydreaming. That's okay; my blankness will add to the thicko persona.

He lumbers through to the shop and I follow behind him. I tell myself that I'm not nervous but I'm lying to myself. My earlier bravado has vanished and I just want to get this shift over with so I can go home and put all of my clothes in the washing machine, put my pyjamas on and watch telly.

'Tash,' Fred booms. 'This is Ellie, she's the new starter and you'll have to show her the ropes.' Introduction made, Fred turns and brushes past me and goes back into the kitchen, leaving me to meet my new work-mate.

The girl leaning against the fryer filing her nails stops mid-file and looks up and stares at me. Huge blue eyes appraise me and I stare back at one of the prettiest girls I've ever seen. Her perfect brows furrow slightly and I'm sure her eyes narrow as she takes in my appearance. I stand immobile like a lumpy, leaden statue.

Just as I expected.

She's going to hate me.

CHAPTER FOUR

I rinse the plate under the running tap water, dry it with the t-towel and put it in the cupboard. I'm leaving for work shortly and could have a free meal there but once I'd noticed Fred's lack of personal hygiene, I couldn't bring myself to eat so much as one chip from that place. Truly disgusting. As well as that, working with the smell of frying food all evening has killed my appetite for chips and anything that goes with it so even getting a takeaway from somewhere else is a no-go. So much for taking advantage of the free meals on offer; I don't think I'll ever be able to eat fried food again.

By the time I get home it's far too late to eat anything – not that I want to – and I've gone straight to bed after a shower so all I've eaten all day is a bowl of porridge in the morning and a sandwich at lunchtime. I eat nothing before I go to work because I can't face it. The hot weather has further dulled my appetite; we've enjoyed a heat wave that has lasted since the beginning of July – two whole weeks of unrelenting hotness. The flat is stuffy and airless but I won't open a window because I'm paranoid that I'll go out and forget to close it. I may be on the third floor but I take no chances.

I've only been working at the chippy for just over a week but I can feel that I've definitely lost weight. My leggings felt loser when I put them on this morning and my face looks different but I can't quite put my finger on exactly what it is that's different about it. I didn't need to lose weight because I wasn't fat, but I can't deny that I'm pleased that my waist is becoming more defined which makes my tits look bigger. Although I'll have to watch that I don't get into the habit of not eating much because I don't want an eating disorder. I've always been careful to not get obsessed about food because I think it would be easy to get enormously fat or go the other way and starve myself to death, because I am, as I've discovered, a person of extremes.

Mimi had an eating disorder. Always overweight, she grew more enormous as each year went by and became fixated on certain types of food which she would eat exclusively for weeks and months on end. She lived entirely on bacon sandwiches and custard creams for several months; another time it was Tesco's chilli con carne ready meals and chocolate digestives.

I don't want to go down that route so I'll have to

watch myself. One of the reasons I don't have any bathroom scales is so that I can't weigh myself and become obsessed by it. But leggings don't lie, do they? Not that anyone will know because I'll still be wearing my normal baggy t-shirt over the top of them.

I give the kitchen worktops a quick wipe over with the dishcloth and fold the t-towel neatly and hang it over the ancient cooker rail and then fold the dishcloth and hang it over the tap. This flat is a damp, falling apart dump but I keep it clean and tidy. I walk around the flat and do my usual leaving routine to check that all the windows are properly closed and securely locked even though I haven't actually opened any of them.

Once I've done it I repeat the process and check them all again to be absolutely certain that they're locked before picking up my bag, pulling the lounge door closed and locking it with the padlock I've fitted. I've made a pretty good job of fixing the hasp onto the door and door frame and I give the padlock a little tug just to satisfy myself that it's locked. I walk down the short hallway – one door to the kitchen, one to my bedroom and one to the bathroom – and step out onto the communal landing and pull the front door closed. I lock both of the locks on the front door and then quickly look around to make sure that no one is watching. Satisfied that I'm alone, I pull my t-shirt up, unzip the money belt secured around my waist and place my keys inside and zip it closed and pull my t-shirt back down to cover it.

My purse and mobile phone are in the lounge as I think they're safer in there rather than carrying them around with me. I have the latest iPhone but I rarely use it to ring anyone as I have no friends, but my life is on that phone and it's extremely precious to me. I can fit it in my money belt if necessary but it's a bit of a squeeze so I prefer to leave it here. Break-ins are few and far between around here because most people have nothing much worth stealing but I'm always nervous when I leave my flat unattended for the evening; another reason why I didn't want a job.

I stride at a brisk pace to the chippy and although the weather is hot, it's overcast and there are no sunbathers lolling around on the green – which means no cat-calls or laughter. When I arrive at the back entrance I nod a greeting to Fred. He's sitting outside the back door on an upended bucket reading the local paper. I continue past him into the kitchen, take my overall out of my bag and hang the bag up on the hook behind the door. I slip the overall over my head, button it up and then go straight through to the serving area of the shop. Tasha is already there and a tall, thin, girl with enormous tits who I haven't met before, is standing next to her.

'Hi, Ellie,' Tasha says with a smile. 'This is Stacey, you two haven't met yet, have you?'

Stacey has been off sick all week with an unspecified illness and hasn't been here since the night I started. I direct a smile in her direction. She stares back at me sullenly while slowly chewing gum open-mouthed and her eyes sweep over me from head to toe. She makes no attempt to hide her appraisal of me, nor the fact that she's not impressed by what she sees. Laughably, before the shop opens, Fred will make her get rid of the chewing gum. He does this to Tash every evening because he says it's not hygienic. The same Fred who never washes and has worn the same apron without washing it for the last twenty years.

I look at Tash who moves slightly away to stand behind Stacey. After a moment she rolls her eyes and pulls a face at me over Stacey's shoulder. I want to laugh but keep my expression impassive as I don't want Stacey to think that I'm laughing at her. I don't want to make an enemy without even trying. Luckily, I've had years of practice at hiding what I'm really thinking.

'Alright?' Stacey eventually mutters quietly and I realise that she's talking to me. This must be what passes for a greeting.

'Yeah, good,' I say. 'Nice to meet you.'

Tash bursts into hoots of laughter and Stacey gives a pig-like snort which I assume is a laugh.

'You're so funny, mate,' Tash says, laughing some more as she comes and stands next to me and puts her hand on my shoulder. 'You're way too posh to work in a chippy.'

I join in the laughter and hope my cheeks aren't as beetroot-coloured as they feel. I have no idea why she thinks I'm posh. I've spent my life saying the wrong thing but luckily, for some unknown reason, Tash seems to like me. I try not to stiffen as she links her arm through mine and leans into me. I'm not used to the casual touch of other people and I feel uncomfortable at her closeness. Mimi never showed affection and even Aaron only bothered when he wanted sex.

When I met Tash on my first shift I assumed she would dislike me as most people do. That first night she was a bit distant and mostly ignored me unless she absolutely had to speak to me but the next night she seemed a lot friendlier. I have very low expectations of people and the most I hope for is that they won't hate me and they'll ignore me and leave me alone. For some reason, the 'popular' ones at school, the pretty ones who all the boys drooled over, were always the worst so I expected this treatment from Tash.

Tash is really pretty and even manages to look good in the disgusting blue nylon overalls that we wear, and I struggle to understand why she's working in a chip shop. She always has a full face of makeup on and does her eyeliner in that cool, flicky way that models do. I think she wears all the makeup because her skin isn't perfect, although the rest of her is. I can see that she has several spots on her chin and forehead which she's covered with thick foundation but it doesn't detract from the fact that she's stunning. Her hair is thick and black – maybe a bit too black to be natural – and she reminds me of the cartoon character Snow White because she often wears a bow in it. She's twenty-one and didn't hide her surprise when I told her I was the same age. Most people take me for older than I am, which I don't mind because then there's no expectation that I'm going to be young and fun or dress fashionably. Aaron said I was more like forty-one than twenty-one; he said going out with me was like going out with his mum.

Being liked is a new experience (I discount Aaron because he wanted something and he was a complete prick) and I can't think *why* she likes me. I usually manage to say the wrong thing but for some reason Tash thinks that I'm witty. Although to be fair, she does most of the talking and I do most of the listening. It's not the first time she's called me posh either, which is hysterical when I think how I was practically dragged up by Mimi. Thank God she never went to my school and didn't know me from there because she wouldn't bother speaking to me if she had; in fact she'd probably refuse to work with me. I think she calls me posh because I can string a sentence together without double negatives and dropping aitches. I keep forgetting that I'm supposed to be playing the complete thicko and to mess everything up. Quite honestly, I don't mind coming here and have actually started to look forward to it. There's only so much loneliness one person can take. And it's nice to have someone laughing with me and not at me for a change.

I wish I was like Tash but I'm not; I could never hope to look like her and I wouldn't even try. Tash has been blessed with good looks and it's a mystery to me why she's ended up here because beauty opens doors that even brains can't. And it's not as if she's stupid either, so I really can't fathom it. When the late night punters come in for their chips she's always getting chatted up and asked out. She always says she has a boyfriend although she's told that she hasn't really, it's just to get rid of unwanted attention.

The good thing is that they're so busy looking at Tash and slobbering over her that most of the time no one even notices me. Although one night a tall, skinny, man with a shaved head and homemade tattoos on his hands tried to chat me up. I gave one-word answers, hoping that he'd take the hint that I wasn't interested. He reminded me of Aaron, although he wasn't anywhere near as good-looking. I just wanted him to take his chips and go but he got nasty when I didn't respond to his pathetic chat up lines and called me a *stuck up bitch*. I ignored him but Tash heard him and ripped into him; told him to *fuck off and crawl under a stone*. I think he was going to have a go at her too before he noticed the two other blokes who'd been chatting her up looking at him with narrowed eyes. He muttered something under his breath and stormed out of the chip shop; he didn't even pick his chips up he was in such a hurry to get away.

No one has ever stuck up for me before; not ever,

except for teachers and the like and they don't count because it's their job and it usually made things worse, anyway. And although I keep telling myself to be a bit more suspicious of Tash, when I think about it logically, there's nothing in it for her by being nice to me so maybe I've met a real, decent person at last. There are some in the world even though I haven't met very many of them. Perhaps it's time I stopped judging everyone by the standard of Aaron and Mimi.

'Stacey and me are going up town tonight, do you wanna come?' Tash asks.

It takes me a minute to realise that she's actually *asking* me if I want to go out with them. I've never been invited anywhere before; I was the kid who was the only one in the class *never* invited to birthday parties.

'Um, what, straight from here?' I ask.

'Yeah.' Tash and Stacey glance at each other and a look passes between them. 'We've bought our stuff to get changed into when we finish. We'll leave our work stuff here and pick it up tomorrow. It'll be well lush; there's a new band on at the Solo Club.'

I don't want to go up town or to the Solo Club. I'm certain it'll be full of people drinking and laughing at me and it'll be just like being back at school.

'I can't,' I say. 'I can't go up town looking like this.' I look down at my clothes.

'That's alright,' Stacey says. 'You don't live far,

do you? We could all go back to yours and get changed.'

'I haven't got anything to wear,' I blurt out.

They stare at me and I rack my brains to think of something to say that'll take the looks of disbelief off their faces.

'I only have really old stuff,' I say. 'And I wouldn't be seen dead in it. I was waiting for my first pay packet to go and buy some new stuff next week.'

'Oh, okay.' Stacey shrugs and resumes her gum chewing and turns away. I see now that I've missed my chance. I don't want to go up town but equally, I don't want to lose Tash's friendship but they won't ask me again. My one chance of actually making friends and I've blown it.

Tash turns to me and leans in close and I smell strawberry shampoo on her hair and minty toothpaste on her breath.

'No worries, come next week,' she says quietly. 'I'll go shopping with you and we can pick some stuff out together. Then next week we can all go to yours straight after work. We could pre-load and have a few drinks before we go up town. What do you reckon?' She looks at me expectantly and I feel relief that she's giving me another chance.

'That'd be great,' I lie. 'I can't wait.'

'Lush,' Tash says. 'It'll be nice not to have to get changed in the shop toilet with Fred perving on us.' She hoots with laughter and Stacey laughs and winks at me as Fred appears at the doorway.

So I'm going, which is bad.

But not as bad as the fact that they're both coming to my flat.

CHAPTER FIVE

I'm meeting Tash at one o'clock outside Primark. I set off for the thirty-minute walk into town at eleven o'clock this morning so that I'd have plenty of time to go to all the banks before meeting her.

I've decided to up the amount that I pay in every week; I think I've been too cautious in paying only three hundred pounds into each account because realistically, why would anyone be watching what I'm doing? I'm not interesting enough that anyone is paying any attention to how much money I have or where it comes from. Three hundred pounds is a piddling amount to most people and it's not as if anyone official has any reason to watch me. If I carry on paying it in at that rate it'll take forever to get it all into the accounts.

I think that years of living with Mimi has made me paranoid; I couldn't breathe without her permission and somehow she always seemed to know if I was even *thinking* of doing something without telling her. I honestly think that she was a witch as well as a bitch. But she's not here anymore and I need to remember that; no one is watching me and no one is remotely interested in me.

So today I've paid in six hundred pounds to one bank, four hundred and fifty in another and five hundred and twenty-five into the others. It would be easier if I had more bank accounts but opening five was difficult enough and to do others I'd have to travel to a different town. Anyone would think that the banks were giving *me* the money to look after and not the other way around the number of forms I had to fill in. Next week I'm going to pay in even more because none of the bank cashiers raised so much as an eyebrow; although I do try to pay in at a different counter with a different person every week if at all possible.

I have a hundred pounds cash to spend on some new clothes when I meet up with Tash which will be more than enough; any more than that would make Tash wonder where I'd got it from. I can't say that I'm looking forward to it; I don't *do* clothes buying and I have an uncomfortable feeling that I'll be expected to get undressed and try stuff on in front of her because that's what normal mates do when they go shopping.

I'm trying to not panic over this and keep reminding myself that when I start my new life I'll have to know how to make friends and blend in with other people otherwise there's no point in *having* a new life. This will be good practice for my new life if nothing else. It's a shame that having gone to the effort to make friends I'll have to leave Tash and Stacey behind but at least I'll know how to make new friends. I need to practice being normal and being with people and if I keep doing it, then perhaps in time, I'll become normal.

Or perhaps not; but I can at least, appear normal.

I can't help feeling nervous about the trying on clothes thing; it's all far too reminiscent of getting changed for PE in the school changing rooms. The only occasion that I ever skived off school was on Tuesday afternoons when it was double PE; tramping around the streets in the rain was preferable to undressing in front of all the other girls and listening to the sniggers and nasty comments about my unflattering, old-fashioned, underwear. Although I always made sure to get my registration mark before I left the school grounds because as I've said before, I'm not stupid.

I've actually spent quite a lot of money this week already, far more than I usually spend. Knowing that Tash and Stacey are intending to come to my flat after work on Saturday threw me into a panic; how could I explain the huge lock and padlock on my lounge door? I couldn't; there's no reason in the world that would explain why I lock my own lounge door when I live alone. After several sleepless nights I had an idea and searched on Amazon and there it was; the answer to my problem. So yesterday morning I took delivery of a top of the range, metal, combination-lock safe. There were cheaper ones on offer but I didn't stint on the cost because I wanted the best.

It's not huge – I would have liked bigger but the one I bought is the biggest that they had. It's very well made and it weighs a ton and I struggled when I man-handled it along the hallway and into my bedroom. I had to take several rests along the way and getting it into the bottom of the wardrobe was particularly difficult. Before it was delivered the Amazon delivery driver rang me and wanted to drop it off at the communal entrance to the flats instead of bringing it up to the third floor. I told him no way and he bought it up on a little wheelie thing and dumped it outside the door and rang the bell; he'd gone before I'd even opened the front door.

Fortunately, the wardrobe in my bedroom is built into the wall which is ideal. I drilled two holes through the floorboards and secured the safe to the floor from the inside with two large bolts. I suppose someone could get it out if they really tried but they'd still have to get it open. Once the wardrobe doors are closed the safe is out of sight and you wouldn't know it was there.

The combination number that I've set to open it is so long that no one will ever guess it. Having a combination for the safe also means that I don't need to carry a key around with me with the possibility of losing it, which is a relief. Quite honestly, I wish I'd thought of it ages ago because it's much better than leaving it all in the lounge. I could have done with it when Aaron lived with me although if he'd seen it, it would have raised too many questions. I never had the lock on the lounge when he was here for the same reason. But of course then I never had a job so I never had to go out and leave him alone so I could keep an eye on him. Although I was always nervous that he'd find it all by accident, the way that I did, and then what would I have done?'

Anyway, no one's going to be able to get that safe open without some sort of serious cutting equipment so it's one less thing to worry about. I couldn't quite fit everything in there but as the cash is going down week by week it won't be a problem for too much longer. I've tucked what I can't fit inside the safe underneath a loose floorboard under the chest of drawers in my bedroom. The carpet is over the top of the floorboard so it's quite undetectable. There's the added bonus that I can leave my phone and purse in the safe without worrying that someone will steal it; much better than carrying it around with me, wedged inside the money belt.

The hasp and bracket on the lounge door took some getting off because I made such a good job of putting them on there. When I'd finally managed to lever it off I took a good portion of the door frame with it. I haven't tried to repair it as I'm not worried that it'll look odd because the rest of the flat is so shabby that it fits right in.

Quarter to one.

I sit down on the bench in the middle of the high street facing the front doors of Primark and wait for Tash to arrive. I've left my phone at home in the safe as I've told Tash that I don't have one; no way do I want her to see my expensive phone because it would cause far too many questions. She was shocked when I told her I was mobile-less as she says she can't live without hers but I told her that I could never afford to have one. She hasn't asked me loads of questions about my circumstances which I'm grateful for but I know all about hers. She lives with her mum in a council house about a ten-minute bus ride in the opposite direction to the chip shop from me. I briefly thought about telling her about Mimi but then stopped myself; if she asks, I'll tell her but if not, I won't. Likewise with Aaron.

Or maybe I won't mention either of them at all.

But I think that in time, she'll probably find out because no one around here can keep their gob shut. Other people's business is an obsession because there's not much else to do, especially as the majority of people don't work. I'm certain that she doesn't know my history yet because if she did, she wouldn't bother with me. She won't want to be tainted by the outcast brush by being a friend to me. Hopefully, by the time she finds out she'll know me a bit better and she'll know that I'm not the retard that everyone takes me for and then maybe she'll overlook my past.

I've had to bring my purse with me today because I needed my cards to pay the cash into the banks. I feel slightly nervous about this because obviously, I can't wedge it in my money belt because Tash will see it when I try clothes on. In desperation, I rummaged around in the back of my wardrobe and found an old handbag of Mimi's that I bought with me when I moved into the flat. God knows why I kept it because it's beyond hideous but it does have the advantage of having a long shoulder strap which I've looped over my shoulder, satchel style, so that no one can snatch it from me. I've hidden all of my bank cards in the zip up pocket of my purse so that they're out of sight and I'll use cash to buy my new clothes.

As I wait for Tash I watch young girls coming out of Primark swinging bulging carrier bags. I usually buy my leggings and T-shirts from here so it's not a new experience for me – but shopping with a friend is.

A friend.

The word sounds strange in my head and I wonder if I can class Stacey as a friend, too. I don't think so, not yet, but maybe in time, who knows? I don't think that Stacey likes me very much and more to the point, I'm not sure that I like her but beggars can't be choosers, can they? I've never had one, never mind two friends in my whole life so I don't know what the friend etiquette is. Do you have to like them or are they just someone to go around with instead of being on your own?

I think maybe you're supposed to like them and have things in common but I'm not going to be fussy because no one is going to have anything in common with me, even if they think they have. Quite honestly, I'll take what I can get.

I didn't like Aaron very much even before he starting throwing his fists around. I did like looking at him at the beginning because he was good-looking but that soon wore off. After a while I couldn't stand the sight of him. I discovered quite quickly that he wasn't very clever and he was also annoying as he didn't realise that he was stupid. He was under the illusion that he was smart and that when he told one of his pathetic jokes he was funny. He couldn't spell or write a sentence without mixing up capital and small letters which just shows his level of thickness.

Even so, I'd decided within the first day of meeting him that I'd put up with him for his looks and for my new *in a relationship* status. I reasoned that having a boyfriend was the normal thing to do and that maybe I wouldn't be such an outcast if I stuck with him. I remember actually thinking, *what have I got to lose?* Lots, as it turned out, but I thought, at the time, that it was better than being on my own and besides, men weren't exactly queuing up at the door to ask me out.

So maybe I'm not as clever as I think I am.

When I leave this life behind me and go far away where no one knows anything about me or my past, I've decided that I'm going to change my name too. It's legal and you can call yourself anything you like because I've looked it up on the internet. It doesn't even cost very much. No more *smelly Ellie* for me. I'm still researching what I'm going to call myself; something a bit up-market, I think, and I'm going to concoct a new previous life history too that doesn't include a psychotic foster mother and a nasty, drug-dealing boyfriend.

Five-to-one.

I'm staring into space wondering what I'm going to buy when I realise that Tash has arrived and is standing outside the travel agents behind me. I don't even have to turn around to see her because I can see her reflection in front of me in Primark's window. She hasn't noticed me and it feels strange being able to watch her like she's in a film. She stands out in her white jeans and pink skimpy top and I sit and admire her. I wish I looked like Tash.

She's deep in conversation with someone, a man, I think, although I can't see him properly because only his jeans and trainers are visible as Primark's window ends where his body begins.

I watch for the next ten minutes as Tash talks to the unseen man before she throws her hands up and shrugs her shoulders and the bit I can see of him moves away. Tash marches across towards the entrance to Primark and is oblivious to the fact that I'm sitting on the bench right on front of her. She strides straight past me without a glance. She stands outside the doors looking down the street and I realise that she's looking for me and wondering where I am. I stand up and saunter over to her and tap her on the shoulder.

'Sorry I'm late,' I say, although I'm not. 'Have you been waiting long?'

'What?' she turns and frowns at me as if she has no idea who I am and I think that maybe she wasn't looking for me, but for someone else, maybe the man that I couldn't see. She stares at me blankly for a moment and just as it's becoming embarrassing she finally manages a smile.

'Oh, hello, mate. Yeah, I've been standing here waiting like a right dick since ten-to-one so let's get on with it.' With that she links her arm through mine, swings me around and we bowl into Primark.

I mentally prepare myself for an afternoon of trying on clothes that I don't want whilst trying to look happy about it but a feeling of uneasiness is bubbling up.

Because I can't help wondering; why is she lying?

CHAPTER SIX

There's a different atmosphere at work tonight and the evening seems to be whizzing by at twice the normal speed. Tash and Stacey seem excited to the point that I wonder if they've been hitting the booze already. I don't remember them being this excited last week and I can't help getting the feeling that I'm being set up for something.

Or maybe it's because I just don't want to go up town.

I definitely don't but I'm committed now; I could get out of it if I really wanted to but that would be the end of my friendship with Tash and any attempt at being a normal person.

I've decided that I don't like Stacey; she has a way of looking at me that is all too reminiscent of Mimi. She clacks chewing-gum around her mouth while staring at me in her dull-eyed way, a bit like a cow chewing the cud, and she only bothers to speak to me when Tash does. I don't trust her but can't put my finger on why. I don't trust anyone, actually, except maybe for Tash just a little bit, because she did stick up for me with the nasty tattooed bloke who came in for his chips.

We finish at ten-thirty tonight which to me, is very late and time to go to bed and far too late to be going out, but according to Tash and Stacey it's far too early to go out up town. They say that the night has barely begun then and that no one bothers getting into town before eleven o'clock as all the clubs are dead before then.

Tash has bought a bottle of Prosecco to drink while we get ready and Stacey has a bottle of voddy in her handbag to top us up when we're in the club. They said that the drinks in the pubs and clubs are an extortionate price and they only ever buy the first one. I don't drink; I don't like the taste and I don't like the feeling of being out of control but I'm not going to tell them that. I'll do what I did with Aaron and tip it away when they're not looking. I had to drink along with Aaron because he was suspicious of anyone who didn't drink alcohol until they couldn't stand up so it was just easier to pretend. By the time he'd had a few lagers I'd wait until he wasn't looking and tip it into his glass; he quite often said that he didn't know why he got pissed so quickly.

'D'ya think your mate can get us into Solo for free,' Stacey asks Tash as she stirs the chips around the wire basket to try and hide the black ones.

'He'll def get me in and maybe one other but if

one of you has to pay we can split it three ways,' Tash says.

Stacey pauses mid-stir and stares at me and I try to ignore her and pretend that I haven't noticed her looking at me. Stacey told me that the clubs like to get the fit girls in early because it helps get the blokes in and they're the ones who spend the most money. I know that it'll be me that has to pay because I'm not fit and no nightclub will let me in for free. I won't ask either of them to split the cost with me though, I'll just pay it.

I might not be fit but Stacey doesn't exactly look great either, but she does have massive tits. The rest of her is skinny to the point of emaciation but her tits are absolutely enormous and tonight she's wearing some sort of push up bra that practically pushes then into your face when you get close to her. She looks like a ten-year-old girl with two balloons strapped to her chest. I wondered if they were fake when I first met her but I don't think they are; not least because there's no way she could afford to get them done and also they're not exactly perky. When she has a normal bra on they're a bit torpedo-shaped and droopy; not like all the celebs with fake ones that look as if they stand up and out to attention without any help at all. The rest of her isn't up to much – sallow skin, thin scrappy hair and a pointy, slightly ratty face. Her teeth are a bit yellow and they slope inwards but none of that matters, because the only thing that men notice about her are her tits.

I'm not jealous of her tits and I'd rather have my own, normal-sized ones because the comments that she gets from the men who come into the chippy are unbelievable. I'd hate the attention and a lot of it is insulting but Stacey laps it up. She's always boasting about her latest one-night stand and what she lets them do to her; it's enough to make you bring your breakfast up. Even Tash mimes sticking her fingers down her throat when Stacey's not looking.

The only bloke who seems to be immune to Stacey's tits is Fred and I think that's because he can't take his eyes off Tash – although it's only when she has her back to him. It's embarrassing in a bloke his age; slobbering over Tash's arse every time she bends over the fryer.

'So what you wearing tonight?' Tash asks Stacey.

Stacey smiles a self-satisfied smile.

'Something new that I got from the market. The blokes are gonna love it. I don't think there's any way I'll be going home on my own tonight.'

I keep my face impassive but inside I cringe; she will shag *anything* that shows her even the slightest bit of attention although they don't seem to come back for more very often.

'What you wearing?' she asks Tash.

'My white jeans and a little white strappy top. Ellie has got white jeans too so were going to be twins.' Tash smiles at me and winks. 'Though her top is black,' she adds.

I smile back at her and try not to feel sick. I have

the same white jeans and white wedge cork-soled sandals and a black top that will barely cover me. I haven't even tried it on as my fears of undressing in front of Tash didn't materialise. My imagined stroll around the shops trying on lots of clothes turned into a mission to get me something to wear in as little time as possible. Tash seemed in a rush and took me straight to the jeans section, held a pair up in front of me and decided they were the right size because she said I looked about the same size as her. She then whisked me to the tops and pulled out the black top and the only thing that I tried on were the pair of cork sandals. Although I was dreading the getting undressed side of things I couldn't help feeling a bit disappointed, plus I'm pretty sure that the jeans won't fit me because Tash is much smaller than me.

Then Tash rushed off; said she had to run some errands for her mum and the next thing I knew I was standing on my own in the queue to pay in Primark. I thought about going and trying the stuff on in the changing room as I was on my own but I couldn't be bothered; I'm hoping the jeans won't fit because then I won't have to wear them. I did get out of the queue and go and get a new bra and a pack of knickers because there's no way I can let Tash and Stacey see the awful underwear that I normally wear. Sports bras and big knickers might be comfy but what normal twenty-one-year-old would wear them? Strange, retarded ones, that's who.

I don't have too much time to dwell on things tonight because the shop's busy. The families coming in early for their tea are replaced by pub regulars who come out of the pub before closing time to get their saveloy and chips to soak the ale up. There's a steady queue and Fred is busy stomping backwards and forwards to the kitchen replenishing the fryers. At ten-fifteen exactly he comes out from the kitchen and goes to the door and turns the sign to closed. Somehow, he always cooks enough to serve the last line of customers and when there are chips left over he reheats them for the early-doors the next day. The chip shop isn't open tomorrow and Monday so I wonder what he does with the leftovers from a Saturday. Probably refries them on Tuesday.

'Evening ladies.' One of the regulars, Jimmy, comes up to the counter on his turn and leans against it. He leers at Stacey's tits and licks his lips and Stacey simpers.

'What can I get you, Jimmy?' Stacey giggles. She thrusts her chest out even more and attempts to sway her skinny hips over to the counter. I see several men waiting in the queue watching her.

'There's an offer,' Jimmy guffaws. 'I'll have you and a side of chips, my lovely.'

Stacey laughs as if it's the funniest thing she's ever heard and I wonder if she'll even make it to the club with us. She's already shagged Jimmy on several occasions; he has a semi-permanent girlfriend and only bothers with Stacey when he's on a break from her. He's grubby-looking and deeply unattractive but Stacey's not fussy. I cross my fingers and hope that she decides to go off with him when we've finished work because I think the evening will be much better without her.

'Salt and vinegar?' Stacey asks, with a wink as she shovels his chips into paper. Fred is next to her moving the fish around the warmer and he doesn't even flinch. Tash and Stacey behave as if Fred isn't there, they don't seem too bothered what they say in front of him because they think he's not listening. I'm not so sure; sometimes I wonder what he's doing on the very many breaks which seem to be mostly spent locked in the grotty toilet out the back.

'Whatever you like, lovely.' Jimmy licks his already moist lips again and I have to look away.

'We're going up town,' Stacey says, as she hands the chips over the counter to him. 'Do you fancy coming?'

'Na, can't, tonight,' Jimmy replies, shoving several chips into his mouth. 'Bit skint at the mo, but you could come to mine instead.'

'Oh.' Stacey looks put out and I can see she's struggling to decide.

'No, I can't,' she says eventually. 'Don't want to let me mates down.'

Jimmy looks annoyed and shrugs.

'Whatever. Your choice.' He turns and heads towards the door.

'Maybe another time,' Stacey calls after him.

'Yeah, I'll think about it,' he says, as he lets himself out of the shop. There are several sniggers from the queue and I put my head down to avoid eye contact with anyone.

'Fucking cheek,' Tash mutters. 'Who does he think he is? You should tell him to do one.'

'I know,' Stacey sighs. 'But I can't, 'cos he's well fit.'

We're at my flat and so far, so good.

Tash and Stacey showed themselves around without even asking me if it was alright which I thought was a bit much. I felt uncomfortable when we were in my bedroom because I wouldn't have put it past one of them to open the wardrobe doors to have a good look inside. I've disguised the safe by putting stuff on top of it but they're so nosy that I don't want to take the chance of them seeing it.

I persuaded them to get ready in the lounge because I said the light's better in here for putting makeup on. Not that Stacey's putting any on; she's ready to go and is knocking back the Prosecco out of a mug as I don't have any wine glasses. Her preparation for our night out consisted of ripping off her overall and t-shirt and leaving her jeans on (which by the way, look pretty grubby and I'm sure she's been wearing them all week) and pulling a bright yellow lycra top over her head. She then took the elastic band out of her hair and scrunched some waxy stuff through it to puff it up a bit. It still looks like rat's tails.

I couldn't take my eyes off her when she took her top off, the bra she was wearing looked several sizes too small and her tits were barely contained but it was the veins all over them that held my attention; fine blue lines running all over the place like a map of the underground. They actually looked painful and it made me wonder if her having massive tits is some sort of illness; that maybe they've had an unnatural growth spurt or something. The yellow top that she's wearing is basically a tube which she's pulled down low so that it just covers her bra but I'm sure I can see the top of her nipples.

'Don't you want some of this, Stace?' Tash holds up the mascara which she's applying to my eyes.

'No, I don't bother. No one looks at me face with these puppies.' She looks down proudly at her chest and swigs another mouthful of Prosecco.

''Okay. Well, I'm nearly done with you, Ellie, I'll just put some stuff in your hair and then you can get your clothes on.' Tash leans into the mirror on the coffee table and checks her own makeup and adds a slick of lip gloss over her lips. She came to work ready made up as usual and is all ready to go. She's put her white jeans and top on and looks amazing. When she got undressed she looked so perfect that I couldn't help wondering again why she's working in a chip shop or why she's bothering to be friends with me. I'm hoping that my jeans don't fit so I can wear my leggings and a t-shirt.

Tash rips the scrunchie out of my hair, making me wince and lets my hair fall loose from its pony tail. She dips her fingers in the pot of hair wax and I guess my hair is about to get the same scrunched-up treatment as Stacey's. It feels strange with her hands pushing and shoving my hair around and it was the same with her doing my makeup; no one ever gets that close to me. Aaron only ever got close when he wanted sex and that was always quick with no affection whatsoever; in fact if he could have done it without touching me, I'm pretty sure he would have.

'There.' Tash stands back and smiles. 'All done. Now put your clothes on and then you can see what you look like.'

I smile as if I'm enjoying myself. Tash doesn't want me to look at myself until I'm totally ready, she says she's doing a make-over on me and that I have to prepare to be amazed. I think that I have to prepare to be horrified but I don't want to spoil it for her so I do as I'm told. I stand up and hurriedly get undressed while she holds my jeans and top ready.

Stacey isn't even looking at me because she's far too interested in pouring herself another Prosecco but I feel really uncomfortable and I can feel myself shrinking downwards just like I used to in the school changing rooms.

'You're lovely and slim,' Tash says. 'Isn't she, Stacey?'

Stacey looks over as I step into the jeans and narrows her eyes at me but says nothing. I hurriedly pull the jeans over my hips and to my surprise they fit perfectly; not the slightest bit too small.

'Okay, now the top,' Stacey says. 'I'll hold it out 'cos you don't want to mess your hair up.'

She holds the top open and I duck down and she pulls it carefully over my head and tugs it down to my waist. It's tight-fitting and it's fortunate that I no longer need to wear my money-belt as there's no way I could wear it underneath without it being obvious.

'Now. Shoes.' Tash places the wedges in front of me and I step into them and am instantly three inches taller. I attempt to walk around and am surprised that they seem quite comfortable.

'Close your eyes,' Tash says. 'Because it's time for the big reveal.'

I close my eyes and she takes my hand and leads me out into the hallway and I shuffle along the hallway with her towards the mirror by the front door. The full-length mirror was already here when I moved in and has age spots sputtered over it. I never use it but haven't bothered to take it down.

'Okay.' Tash grabs my shoulders and manoeuvres me around. 'When I say the word you can open your eyes.'

'Okay.'

'Ready? One, two, three, open!'

I open my eyes and stare at the stranger in the mirror.

Oh. My. God.

CHAPTER SEVEN

I can't stop looking at myself; as we walk down the high street I keep looking at my reflection in the shop windows because I can't believe that what I'm seeing is me.

When Tash told me to open my eyes, I looked in the mirror and it took me several minutes to realise that I was seeing myself. I know that sounds ridiculous but I look so different – I look like another person.

I look *hot*.

For the first time in my life I liked what I saw reflected back at me. The makeup is maybe a bit too much and the clothes are cheap-looking, but there's no denying that I look like a pretty twenty-one year-old instead of the frumpy *who knows what age she is and who gives a shit* mess that I usually look.

I'm slim and actually have a figure with tits and a waist and am a very similar build to Tash. The features that I've always hated and thought of as dull and non-descript now seem petite, although my eyes seem huge. Tash has overdone the mascara and eye shadow but I made sure to thank her even though Stacey was very sniffy about it. Tash kept saying to her how great I looked but Stacey wouldn't agree; she just shrugged her shoulders and clacked the gum around her mouth.

When we arrived at the King's Arms there were plenty of free tables but Tash said that we'd stand at the bar because who wants to hide away at a corner table where no one can see us? I know she means that she wants men to notice us. The three of us are drinking pints of cider because Tash says it's the cheapest drink going and it'll last longer than a vodka and coke. I don't like the taste and am only taking tiny sips because it feels as if it's gone straight to my head even though I've hardly drunk any of it.

'That guy's eyeing you up,' Tash says, nudging my elbow.

I follow the direction of her gaze to see a tall, dark-haired guy staring at me. He catches my eye and winks and raises his glass and I feel my face grow hot.

'See?' Tash giggles. 'Told you so.'

'Maybe he's looking at you,' I say.

'No, it's defo you. You'll be fighting 'em off now you've had your makeover, won't she, Stacey?' Tash stares pointedly at Stacey who drains the rest of her cider and bangs it down on the bar.

'For fuck's sake Tash, give it a rest,' Stacey says.

'It's only a bit of makeup. A bit of slap can make even the most banged up face look decent.'

Tash looks annoyed and Stacey gives a spiteful smile.

'Why don't you try it then, Stacey?' I ask, surprising myself.

'What?' Stacey asks with a frown.

'A bit of slap?' I suggest. 'Maybe it'll work for you 'cos your face is a bit banged up. It could do with a bit of help.'

Stacey stares at me in shock and for a moment I think she might hit me. I'm shocked at myself; I don't do confrontation, it's not my style at all. I think it's the cider; it's gone straight to my head and mouth.

'Why are you so fucking rude, *Ellie*?' Stacey asks.

'Don't know,' I retort. 'Why are you?'

We face each other and Stacey steps closer and I can smell the sour smell of her perspiration. I should back down but I find that I can't; I don't think there's any chance that Stacey's going to want to be my friend after this but I don't care.

'Hey, come on,' Tash steps between us and pushes us both apart. 'Let's not spoil the night. How about we drink up and head to the club?'

I stare at Stacey and she stares back before dropping her gaze and I feel a moment of triumph that I've won; I've made her back down first.

'Okay,' Stacey says. 'Let's go.'

Tash drinks the rest of her cider and I pick mine up and take a sip before putting it back down on the bar.

'I don't want that,' I say. 'I'm ready.'

Stacey leans across me and grabs my glass from the bar and gulps the cider down in three swallows whilst glaring at me over the top of the glass. She's the same at work; she can demolish a bag of chips in about two seconds yet there's not an ounce of fat on her aside from her tits; everything she eats and drinks must go straight to her chest.

Tash leads the way and Stacey and I follow behind in a line and snake our way through the throng to the doors. Am I imagining it or can I feel the dark-hair guy's eyes on me? As we reach the doors I turn around and look over to the bar to see if I can see him. He's not there and I realise that I seriously need to get over myself; a bit of slap and some Primark clobber and I suddenly think that I'm God's gift to men. I feel immediately deflated and then realise that the reason I can't see him at the bar is because he and his mates are just behind us on their way out of the pub.

'Come on, Ellie,' Tash says. 'We need to get there soon or else we'll have to pay to get in.'

'I'm coming.' I turn my head back to the front and we head out of the doors. I think I may even attempt a bit of a wiggle as we march up the high street towards the Solo Club just in case dark-haired guy might be behind us. Don't get me wrong, there's no way I want another boyfriend because Aaron was enough to put me off for a very long time but there's nothing wrong in being wanted, is there?

We arrive outside the Solo Club and there's a huge, man-mountain of a bouncer bursting out of his black jacket standing on the door. He greets Tash with a smile and a kiss and makes no secret of the fact the he's looking me up and down. After a whispered conversation with Tash – all done while he's having a grope of her arse which she doesn't seem to mind – he agrees to let me and Tash in but says he can't stretch to three free entries and Stacey will have to pay. I try to keep the smile off my face – okay, maybe I don't try *that* hard – and after Stacey hands over a tenner to the girl at the desk we descend down the steep stairs and into the darkness of the Solo Club. The music is booming and has so much base that the floor feels as if it's vibrating up through my feet. There are a lot of people in here already and I'm sure that heads turn in our direction as we make our entrance.

'Stick your tits and bums out, girls,' Tash shouts over the music. 'This is where the party starts.'

No one's laughing at you, I keep reminding myself. I straighten my shoulders and follow Tash and Stacey towards the bar and wait while Tash shouts our order to the barman. We're barely got our drinks in our hands before Stacey heads towards the dance floor. She doesn't ask if we want to join her. The dance floor is a tiny patch of coloured flooring with lights set around the edges and is no bigger than my kitchen. Tash and I trail after her and stand at the side and watch.

Stacey is the only one dancing.

She doesn't care, in fact I'd say that she's enjoying being the centre of attention. After the first track finishes her dancing progresses from wiggling around on the spot to an attempt at what looks like twerking. A group of lads with bottles in their hands are standing at the side cheering her on and she's really going for it, so much so that any minute her tits are going to break free from the yellow top and hit her in the face. We stand watching this excruciating floor show for less than ten minutes and I decide that I've already had enough.

'Shall we go to the bar?' Tash shouts in my ear.

'Okay,' I shout back, although I still have a vodka and coke in my hand that I haven't taken so much as a sip out of. 'What about Stacey, should we ask her to come with us?'

'Fuck no,' Stacey snorts. 'I don't want blokes thinking we're with *that*. Let's go and stand at the bar and with a bit of luck she'll forget about us and cop off with one of those losers. We'll make sure we dance well away from her.' She turns and heads towards the bar and I follow her. I hear whoops and whistles from behind me from the group of lads gathered around the dance floor and I look over my shoulder to see that Stacey is in the process of doing a slut drop to the floor. There's a guy standing in front of her gyrating his hips and thrusting his groin towards her and with each thrust the lads shout and whoop louder. Stacey's loving the attention and for a moment I almost feel sorry for her; she doesn't seem to care that they're only after sex and will use her and discard her like a used condom. The feeling of sympathy is only fleeting though because I soon remember that no one has ever felt sorry for me, ever. Besides, Stacey's not very nice and doesn't even like me so why should I give a shit that men treat her like dirt? Stacey wasn't at my school but if she was I'm quite sure that she'd have been one of the kids calling me names, so why waste my sympathy on her?

There's a crush when we reach the bar and Tash knocks back her drink and gets in the queue for another. I thought that we were only buying one drink but Stacey has the voddy in her handbag so it looks like we have no choice. Not that I'm bothered; I didn't pay to get in so I can afford it.

As Tash waits to be served I decide that I'm going to drink this vodka because at some point I'm going to be expected to dance and there's no way I can do that completely sober. I raise the glass and drink it straight down; I can barely taste the vodka but I feel the hit almost immediately. I've never danced before but I'm sure I can manage some sort of side to side shuffle; there's no need for me to do a Stacey slut drop.

'What are you giggling at?' Tash shouts over the music, turning towards me.

I wasn't even aware that I was giggling; maybe it was the thought of me doing a slut drop.

'I was laughing at the bloke dancing with Stacey,' I lie. 'He looks completely out of it.'

Tash rolls her eyes.

'What a slag,' she says with disgust. 'I don't want her coming out with us again. Don't want everyone thinking we're like her.'

So Tash is no friend of Stacey's; I'm a little surprised and maybe a bit disappointed. Even though I don't like Stacey it tells me that if Tash knew me and my history, she wouldn't want to be my friend either.

Tash orders our drinks and then turns and hands me mine.

'I got us doubles, it'll save queuing again,' she shouts, as she hands it to me. 'As it's your first night out I thought I'd treat us.'

'Thanks,' I say, having no intention of drinking it.

'Let's go and dance but get as far away from that slag as you can,' Tash says.

I nod and lead the way.

Here goes nothing.

I'm dancing.

I'm dancing and no one is pointing at me and laughing. I started off doing a side-to-side shuffle and when that didn't go too badly I threw in a little hip wiggle that Tash does a lot of. I don't feel stupid and I don't feel like I'm making a fool of myself.

I drank the double voddy.

I didn't intend to but it was easier to drink than dance with it in my hand and I feel better for it – but I won't have any more. If Tash insists on buying more I'll take it but I'll throw it on the floor when she's not looking. There are so many drinks spilled on the carpet that one more won't notice. I've even had a few blokes try to chat me up – not that I can hear what they're saying because the music is so loud but it makes me feel good; like a normal person.

Stacey has disappeared, no doubt with one or all of the jeering gang of blokes watching her. The evening is going way better than I thought it would and I'm just thinking what a great night it's turned out to be when something, of course, has to spoil it.

A guy jigs across from the side of me and jiggles about in front of me and smiles. My answering smile is frozen in position when I realise that I know who it is. It's Oobie, Aaron's best friend. Just about the last person in the world that I wanted to bump into.

I go through the motions of dancing and try to keep the horror from my face. Oobie leans in close and I turn my head to try and hear what he's saying above the thump of the music.

'I said,' he shouts, when I don't hear him the first time. 'What's your name? I haven't seen you here before.'

The relief is immense; he has no clue who I

am and who can blame him? I barely recognised myself in the mirror so why should he?

'Jess,' I answer, saying the first name that pops into my head. 'What's yours?'

'Oobie,' he shouts with a grin. 'And I come here all the time.'

'Hi Oobie,' I shout over the music as the beat increases and we dance even faster. 'It's all new to me. I'm a first timer.'

Well, the first time since the night Aaron died.

CHAPTER EIGHT

The Solo Club was one of Aaron's favourite haunts; not that he ever took me there. The darkness and pounding music are a good camouflage for dealing drugs as is the emergency exit to the car park for a quick getaway in the event of a police raid. At the weekend the place was always rammed, he told me, with a steady flow of customers eager to try whatever latest designer drug he had to peddle.

When I first met Aaron I had no idea he was a drug dealer – just as I had no idea that he was a lying, cheating, vicious, nasty piece of work. Laughably, I thought he was one of the normal, harmless, work-shy, beer-drinking layabouts who live on the estate.

I never actually told Aaron that he could move into my flat and I never wanted him to but somehow, it just happened. In hindsight I think that he targeted me because I had a flat and he needed somewhere to stay; not very flattering, is it? He was living with 'a mate', or so he told me. I never actually went to his place so he was probably lying about that as well as everything else; he could have been sleeping rough for all I know.

When we'd been together for a couple of weeks, he stayed over at mine for the night. He was actually okay to me then and I thought he was a decent kind of guy. I wasn't in love with him or anything, I just thought it was better than being on my own. He told me he was moving in with another mate and asked if he could stay at mine for a couple of nights because he had to wait for someone to move out before he could move in. What could I say? It would have sounded mean to say no and I thought, a couple of nights is do-able. At first I quite liked it because it was better than being on my own all the time and he was appreciative when I cooked him a meal and played house. It was novel and new and was only going to be a temporary arrangement, so where was the harm?

Except that it wasn't temporary; once he'd moved in he never left and it wasn't long before he stopped being nice to me and started treating my flat as if it belonged to him and not to me. On the nights when he wasn't going out he'd have all his mates round and they'd take over the lounge – which made me very nervous – and sit in there all night drinking wife-beater and stinking the place out with their joints and farts.

I didn't want to join them, which was just as

well because I wasn't invited; not even in my own home. After a few weeks of putting up with it I plucked up the courage and told Aaron that he had to leave and that I didn't want him living with me anymore. His reply?

A fist in the face.

It was completely unexpected and shocking. I knew by then that he wasn't very nice but I never realised that he was violent. I thought that he'd broken my nose because it hurt so much but as the swelling subsided I realised that luckily, he hadn't, although I did have two black eyes.

Aaron said that if I didn't want to live with him anymore that was okay, he didn't have a problem with that but I would be the one leaving and not him. He said that he had just as much right to a council flat as me and that it wasn't fair that I'd jumped the waiting list because I was a retard that social services had decided to look after. I realised then that I'd made a monumental mistake in letting him in and I had no idea how to get rid of him. I considered contacting social services because it was true, they had got me the flat after Mimi died but it was only so they could move a family into Mimi's old house and not have me living in a three bedroom house on my own. The only thing that stopped me was that I knew that once I'd involved them, I'd never be rid of them.

So my life turned into one of fetching, carrying and cooking for Aaron and trying my best not to antagonise him when he'd had a skin-full. It was like living with Mimi all over again.

When his mates came round I'd sit in my bedroom while they whooped it up in my lounge and made a mess that I'd have to clear up the next day. And all the time they were sitting in there I was as nervous as hell. I didn't know how much longer I'd be able to stand it but had no idea what to do about it. I knew that like Mimi, life would be much easier without Aaron in it but I let the situation linger on because I'm not good at making decisions – at least, I never used to be – when two things happened that meant I had to do something and do it soon.

Firstly, I discovered that Aaron was dealing drugs. I think on some level that I knew this already but it hadn't really sunk in. When he made a big thing of keeping his 'stash' under the bath behind the bath panel I knew that I had to wake up. He warned me that if the police turned up I was to say that he didn't live with me and had no idea where he was. I thought this over and realised how bad this could be for me, because what if the police turned up and searched the flat? All of my plans would be ruined and I'd be asked to do some explaining of my own. Even if I told them the truth, why would they believe me? They'd think that any money they found in this flat was drug money and it would all be confiscated and I'd never see any of it again.

That would be it; all my hopes of starting a new life would be over.

I was digesting this fact and deciding what to do when the second thing happened and I knew that I couldn't put off making a decision any longer. Aaron gave me a particularly vicious beating – not that it was apparent to anyone else, even if they'd bothered to look at me, because by this time he'd learned not to leave bruises where people could see them – because I'd accidently burned the plastic pattern off his favourite sweatshirt with the iron. I'd only burned it because he was going on at me and I wasn't concentrating properly. I know that the burned sweatshirt was just an excuse; he was in a foul mood for some reason and I was going to be made to pay for his bad mood come what may. If it hadn't been the sweatshirt he would have found another excuse like me looking at him funny or something.

I'd got used to his abuse by then and there wasn't a week went by that he didn't vent his anger on me in some way; a twisted arm or a Chinese burn. Hair-pulling was also a favourite of his and I had quite a few bald patches where he'd pulled it so hard it had come out by the roots. But the latest beating was much worse and my ribs hurt when I breathed in and I think he may have cracked them. Like Mimi before him, I was afraid that one day he might kill me.

And just as it was with Mimi, it was a fact that my life would be so much better if he wasn't around anymore. And once I'd had that thought, well, the rest of it was easy once I'd figured out how to do it.

I had to kill him, there was no doubt about that, and one of the easiest ways would be to wait until he passed out into his usual drunken, unconscious sleep and stab him. I gave this serious consideration and on several nights I stood over him whilst he was sleeping with the large butcher's knife in my hand that I'd brought from the market. It would have been so easy to plunge that knife into his chest, and also immensely satisfying because I hated him so much by then. But each time I managed to stop myself because the truth of it was, I didn't want to go to prison.

I could hardly claim self-defence if I stabbed him while he was asleep. There was no way I could stab him when he was awake because he'd easily overpower me as he was so much bigger than me. I shuddered at the thought of what he would do to me with a knife.

No, whichever way I killed him it had to be totally risk free with no possibility of him attacking me. I also had to make sure that I would never be caught and sent to prison for it.

The solution, when it came to me was quite simple and also, I decided, poetic justice. I waited until he was passed out on the sofa one night and then locked myself in the bathroom, removed the bath panel and pulled out his stash. It was a hefty plastic bag full of white pills with another bag full of tiny wraps of white powder which I knew was cocaine. I ignored the cocaine as I had no use for it and opened the bag of pills. I took ten of them out and wrapped them up in the foil that I'd taken into the bathroom with me. I replaced his stash in exactly the same position that I'd found it and put the bath panel back. I was sweating by the time I came out of the bathroom and it wasn't from the heat.

I'm not sure what the pills were but I'd heard Aaron telling his mates to only take one pill or a half if they were going to drink as well because they were 'good stuff'. I'm not sure what ten pills would do to someone but I was hoping that the outcome wouldn't be good. I didn't even feel bad about what I was going to do because I had no choice and he deserved it.

He more than deserved it.

Getting him to take the tablets wasn't going to be a problem because they were tiny and all I needed to do was crush them up and drop them into a bottle of lager and he'd drink it down without even noticing. The question was, where was I going to do it, because no way did I want him overdosing in my flat which would bring unwanted police attention to my door.

And I didn't even need to figure it out because Aaron had already given me the answer himself. When he was drunk, he couldn't resist bragging to me how clever he was; he thought I was so stupid and scared of him that I wouldn't dare tell anyone else – and he was right.

Not that there was anyone to tell.

He told me many times how the Solo Club was made for dealing. Everyone in the club used the fire exit to go outside for a smoke and he'd go out there and deal; it was perfect because there were no cameras and no prying eyes. He bragged that he slipped the bouncers a few quid just in case they noticed so they'd turn a blind eye to his dealing. It was money for old rope, he said, and he couldn't sell the stuff quick enough.

So I waited until the following Saturday night and I went to the back of the Solo Club and hid at the back of the car park so I could have a look at the place and plan what I was going to do. It couldn't have worked out better because several of the bar staff came out on their breaks for a fag and I noticed that they all wore the same – jeans, black t-shirt and a black baseball cap with the Solo Club logo on it. I didn't have a Solo Club baseball cap but I figured that for my purposes, a plain black one would do.

I went back home and for the next week I was like a cat on hot bricks; now that I had a plan I just wanted to get it done. Every time Aaron was horrible to me, which was pretty much all of the time, I had to stop myself from smiling because I knew that come Saturday night/Sunday morning, he was going to be dead or at the very least, a vegetable. I would prefer him dead but I wasn't fussy, although I didn't want to cause the NHS the expense of keeping him alive indefinitely.

Saturday night arrived and Aaron seemed to be

hanging around the flat forever and I thought he'd never leave. He always went out on a Saturday night and I couldn't understand it. Did he, like Mimi, have a sixth sense, did he somehow know what I had planned? I couldn't see how he possibly could but such were the state of my nerves by then that I'd convinced myself that he'd guessed what I was going to do. I'd finally given up hope of ever getting rid of him, when he threw down the remote control, retrieved his stash from the bathroom and left the flat without a word.

I waited until it was nearly one o'clock in the morning and then I set off on the walk into town. I wore jeans and a black t-shirt and I had a black baseball cap tucked into my back pocket. When I got to the car park at the back of the club I put the cap on and tucked my hair up inside it. Using one of Aaron's many lighters that I'd bought with me, I lit up one of the cigarettes that I'd pinched out of Aaron's packet – it was disgusting, God knows why people smoke – and I casually ambled over and joined the back of the group of people standing outside the fire exit. No one even noticed me and when I was sure no one was watching I sauntered into the club and started collecting empty glasses and bottles from the tables whilst looking around for Aaron.

I soon spotted him; he was lounging against the wall opposite the dance floor with a bottle of lager in his hand. I manoeuvred my way around the room until I was standing behind him in the corner. I couldn't see his regular mates and that concerned me; they wouldn't be looking for me and my baseball cap was a good disguise but I wanted them where I could see them. Oobie suddenly appeared in front of Aaron with two bottles of lager in each hand and he handed two to Aaron. I held my breath as Aaron stretched his arm out behind him and propped them both on the narrow ledge that ran around the room.

Honestly, I couldn't have asked for anything better, it was like it was meant to be. It was the work of mere seconds to tip the ready-crushed contents from the piece of foil into one of the lager bottles. Aaron and Oobie had no idea I was even there.

The hardest part was waiting and watching to make sure that he drank it. I may be a murderer but I didn't want an innocent person to die, it had to be *him*. I didn't have to wait very long before he drank it; he finished the bottle in his hand and then leaned behind and picked up the next one and drained it in about three swallows because he was a greedy pig as well as being vile. When he'd finished and put the bottle behind him and picked up the next one I took the empty bottle from the ledge and tucked it underneath my sweatshirt. I then casually moved back around the room and left the way that I'd come; through the fire exit.

I don't know how long it took him to die but before I'd walked half-way home I heard the sirens of the ambulance. Two sirens, actually, so maybe one of them was the police.

I may be a murderer but I'm not all bad, I did my bit for the environment and threw the lager bottle into the bottle bank in the recycling area before I went up to my flat. It made a very satisfying sound as it hit the bottom and shattered into hundreds of pieces.

It was several days before I found out for sure that he was dead when his mate Oobie turned up at the front door. I didn't want to let him in but felt that I had to sp that I'd look like the grieving girlfriend.

Oobie seemed more concerned about using the bathroom than anything else. I think he was checking behind the bath panel for Aaron's stash because he was in there for quite a while. I asked him what had happened and he said *Aaron had taken some bad shit*. He didn't seem particularly sad and I remembered then that Aaron used to treat him like shit, too. I couldn't manage to squeeze out any tears but I did play the dumb, disbelieving girlfriend quite well – not that Oobie was the slightest bit interested; once he'd been in the bathroom he couldn't wait to get away. As he left he said he'd let me know when the funeral was but he never did – which was just as well because I had no intention of going.

After I'd closed the door on him I gathered up Aaron's clothes that were scattered around the place and put them into a bin bag and took them down to the bins. I would have liked to have burned them really but I didn't have anywhere to do it; it would have felt good to see it all go up in smoke.

Good riddance to bad rubbish.

Then I went back up to the flat and got my purse and went to B&Q and bought a new lock for the front door because I didn't know how many keys to my flat might be floating around. I bought the hasp and padlock for the lounge at the same time so I was quite busy the next day. I had to YouTube how to do it and go out and buy some tools as well.

So. Job done.

One less bastard in the world.

CHAPTER NINE

The sunlight streaming through the flimsy bedroom curtains wakes me and I slowly open my eyes. I wince as I move my head to see what the time is on the clock on the bedside table. My brain seems to be rattling. Is it possible for a brain to rattle? It certainly feels like it and I wonder if I've done myself some permanent damage. The clock tells me that it's nearly one o'clock and I can't believe that I've slept so long. I don't feel that I've been asleep; I feel as if I've been unconscious.

How much did I drink last night? I can definitely remember drinking three vodka and cokes but after that it's a blank. I have no recollection of getting home or of going to bed. Surely three drinks wouldn't cause a memory black out?

The mound underneath the duvet next to me stirs and I slide silently sideways out of bed and step quietly across the room to the door, stumbling over my discarded jeans that are strewn on the floor in the process. My bladder feels as if it's about to burst and I have the most foul taste in my mouth but strangely, no headache. I pad bare-foot down the hall to the bathroom and close the door and lock it.

What happened last night?

I pull down my pants and flop down onto the toilet with relief; I'm still wearing my bra and top from last night as well as my pants so thankfully I didn't lose all inhibitions. As I pee I rack my brains to try and remember the events of the night but I draw a complete blank. The last thing I can remember with any certainty is dancing with Oobie and feeling rather pleased with myself that he had no idea who I was. I have a vague memory of Tash dancing toward us with another drink for me and Oobie smiling at her. I remember that the thought was in my head that I'd never realised how attractive Oobie was when he was with Aaron but that I needed to be careful and not get over-confident.

After that I have only snapshots of the night; Oobie holding mine and Tash's hands as we twirled around him on the dance floor, Tash laughing uncontrollably – at what, I have no idea, and Stacey, stumbling around the club in tears, dishevelled and muddy with ripped jeans and a broken bra-strap, the bouncer telling her she had to leave because she was drunk.

After that, nothing, no matter how hard I try to remember.

I stand up and pull up my pants and consider getting into the shower; tempting, but I'll have to go back to the bedroom first to get some clothes. I flush the toilet and put the seat down and sit back down on it while I think about what to do. The worse thing about the blackout is that I have no idea who I shared a bed with last night; no recollection at all of who is underneath the duvet.

Is it Oobie?

I can't remember; the good thing is that I still have my clothes on so I don't think I've had sex with whoever it is but the very bad thing is that I was so out of it, who knows what I might have said to them. I could have bragged about Aaron and Mimi, of my plans for the future, who knows? I normally keep everything to myself but I felt different last night after just a couple of drinks so who knows what I might have done.

I can't hide in the bathroom all day so I stand up and grab my dressing gown from the hook on the back of the door and tie it around me.

There's only one way to find out.

I stand at the sink and brush my teeth and then take a flannel to my face and the remains of last night's makeup. The mascara in particular takes some getting off and my face is red and shiny by the time I've finished. I'd like to say I feel better but I don't; I feel fuzzy-headed and slightly out of it and if this is what hangovers are like I won't be drinking again. I quietly open the bathroom down and walk silently down the hall to my bedroom and stand at the doorway and look over at the bed; the mound hasn't moved and the duvet is piled high over the head of whoever is in the bed.

I really want to look inside the wardrobe to make sure that the safe is still locked but knowing my luck, whoever is in bed will choose that moment to wake up. I stand in an agony of indecision and then decide that I'll open the wardrobe door and get some clean clothes out and have a look at the same time.

I open the wardrobe door and it makes its usual squeaking sound but there's no movement from the bed. I grab some leggings from a hanger and bend down and reach into the back of the wardrobe and take a t-shirt from the pile that's sitting on top of the safe. The bottom t-shirt is draped over the front of the safe and I pull it sideways to reveal that the safe is closed. I stand up and close the wardrobe door with relief.

The mound underneath the duvet still hasn't moved and I make the decision to take a shower and get dressed before I confront them. I'll feel much more in control with my clothes on and maybe a shower will stir the memories of what happened last night. I quietly pull open the top drawer of the chest of drawers and pull out clean underwear and then retrace my steps to the bathroom.

I lock the door and turn the rusting old shower on to the cold setting, strip off the dressing gown and underwear and step underneath the water.

Time to wake up.

I have to grit my teeth to stay underneath the freezing water and I can only stand it for a few minutes before I turn the tap to hot. I wash my hair and soap myself up and by the time I step out of the shower I still don't remember any more about last night but I do feel more awake. I throw all of my dirty clothes into the laundry basket and once I'm dressed I go into my bedroom and look over at the bed.

No movement at all.

The thought pops into my head that whoever is underneath the duvet is dead and that I murdered them last night, because it wouldn't be the first time, would it?

My heart starts to race and I feel as if I'm going to have a heart attack until I remember that they definitely moved this morning when I woke up so they weren't dead then. Why would I kill them? It's not as if I'm a violent person going around looking for people to murder; I'm not Dennis Neilsen for fuck's sake. I need to stop my imagination running way with itself and get a grip. I should step over there right now and pull the duvet back to see who's spent the night sleeping in my bed.

But I don't because I haven't got the guts.

I turn and go out into hall and along to the kitchen and fill the kettle from the tap and put it on to boil. I go to get a mug out of the cupboard but there are none in there; this is when I notice the three mugs on the draining board and three more in the sink which is the sum total of my mug collection. Three and three makes six; Tash, Stacey and I used three of them to drink our Prosecco out of before we went out. The other three must have been when we got back which means there were three of us. Did Stacey come back here for some reason? A blurred memory nudges the edge of my brain but disappears before I can grasp hold of it. The empty Prosecco bottle is still on the draining board where Stacey left it and there's a half empty bottle of something called Moscow Mule standing next to it. I pick the bottle up and unscrew the lid and sniff it and my stomach rolls in protest; it's a weird radioactive blue colour and smells a bit like disinfectant. I'm screwing the top back on and wondering who the third mug was for when a voice from the doorway interrupts my thoughts.

'Christ, not getting on it already, are you?'

I had to wash the mugs up before I could make a coffee and Tash spent the whole time that I was doing so telling me not to make so much noise. I made us some toast and we're now sat at the chipped Formica-topped kitchen table tucking into it. Tash says she feels like death but she doesn't look like it, aside from her panda eyes where her mascara has smudged, she looks fine. Even the clothes that she wore last night don't look like she's slept in them even though she has. I've noticed this about some people; they can make no effort and wear the same stuff for days on end and still look fine and fresh.

I felt so much better when I saw it was Tash that had slept in my bed next to me and not Oobie or some other random man. Although I'm being very careful what I say to her because I'm trying to find out if I've told her anything that I shouldn't have.

'I feel better now I've had something to eat,' Tash says, shoving the last piece of toast into her mouth.

'Me too,' I say.

'Good night, though, wasn't it mate?' Tash says.

'It was,' I agree. 'Though I can't remember that much about it, if I'm honest.'

Tash laughs.

'I'm not surprised, the amount you drank. I thought I could drink but bloody hell, you can pack it away. If you hadn't passed out I think you'd have finished the Moscow Mule on your own.'

'I passed out?'

'Yeah pretty much, I helped you into bed and you went out like a light.'

I wonder if I pulled my jeans off or Tash did; I decide not to ask.

'So who else came back here?' I ask. 'Was it Stacey?'

'Stacey?' Tash frowns. 'I don't know where Stacey was but she wasn't here, she got thrown out of the club and I never saw her after that. She was in a right state; off her head. Stupid cow. No, it was just you and me here, mate, no one else.'

'Yeah, I remember her getting thrown out, couldn't remember if we met up with her again. I just wondered who used the other mug.'

'Other mug?' Tash shrugs. 'I dunno, one of us probably, we were pissed, remember.'

'We were,' I say. 'So pissed that I don't even remember getting home, the last thing I remember is dancing and having a good time.'

'Booze does that to me if I have too much,' Tash laughs. 'I try to stop before I get to the point where I do something I wish I hadn't.'

I wish I'd stopped, I don't like the feeling of not remembering what I've done, of a lost night without any memory. If that's what being pissed does for you, you can keep it.

'Thanks for letting me stay over last night,' Tash says. 'My mum would have gone mad if I'd gone home in that state. I might be twenty-one but she still thinks she can tell me what to do 'cos I'm living under her roof, as she puts it.'

I smile and hope that now she's eaten her toast she'll leave. I know that I need to have friends and be normal but that doesn't mean I want her hanging around all day. I want her to leave so I can tidy my flat up and change the bed and put my washing on, but most importantly, I want to check the safe to make sure that nothing is missing. I know that realistically, nothing *can* be missing but I need to reassure myself.

Tash leans back in the chair and stretches.

'It's going to be so much fun, mate,' she says, with a yawn.

'What is?' I ask.

'You and me,' she says. 'We can have parties and mates round – though not skanky Stacey – life's going to be one long party. Plus I won't have to get a bus to work no more.'

I stare at her and attempt to keep the horror from my face.

'I'll have to break it to my mum gently, though,' she continues. 'Cos she'll proper miss me but it's gonna be great. Thanks so much for asking me to move in.'

I have no recollection of asking her, none at all, but I must have done, mustn't I?

The big question now is, how am I going to un-ask her?

CHAPTER TEN

I didn't murder Mimi, although there were many times that I wanted to. Although there is the possibility that I could have saved her but I chose not to, so that's a sort of murder, isn't it?

Like Aaron, Mimi deserved to die, but unlike Aaron, I didn't engineer her death, fate did.

With hindsight I now realise that what's happened in my life is that I've gone along with things and done what other people wanted because I thought that I had no choice. I've spent my life thinking that because of my situation I just had to try and stay out of everyone's way and not annoy them and I'd be allowed to carry on living. Don't make any fuss and be thankful to be left alone by people to live my sorry excuse for a life.

After I left school my life continued in much the same way as it had before except that I no longer had to endure school and all of the people in it. This would have been a blessing except that it meant that I had to suffer Mimi for twenty-four hours a day. I'm not sure which was worse. I'd have a few hours respite from her with the shopping and stuff but mostly it was just me and her stuck in the house. I wasn't a little kid anymore but I was still terrified of her and would do my utmost to avoid upsetting her.

It wasn't that she was even physically violent to me very often and looking back, I'm sure I could have overpowered her because I was younger and fitter even though she was much bigger – but the thought never crossed my mind. I thought that she would live forever and that I would look after her when she got old. That was the way that my life was going to be. I never thought beyond that; I never thought of being on my own and actually having a life.

I had my books which transported me to other worlds and I'd bought myself a second-hand television for my bedroom so life, if you could call it that, was bearable as long as I didn't compare my existence to anyone else's.

Mimi would sit in the same chair in the lounge all day before she lumbered up the stairs to bed in the early hours and I'd fetch and carry for her and cook whatever she wanted to eat.

She didn't go out very much by then because she'd got so huge that her legs were so fat that they rubbed together. It was hard work for her to walk anywhere and much easier to send me out for everything. The only place she ever went every week, without fail, was into town and, as I discovered, to the bank. She never allowed me to go with her and I only knew she went to the bank because I followed her one day to see where she was going. Whenever I did the shopping she would give me cash because she didn't trust me with her bank card.

I didn't like it when she decided to go out; it made me feel threatened and I was afraid that she'd decide that she didn't need me anymore. Mimi told me on many occasions that she was only letting me live with her out of the goodness of her heart. I was terrified that she'd decide she'd had enough of me and throw me out onto the streets. Social Services hadn't bothered with me since I'd turned eighteen and Mimi told me that they wouldn't; I was on my own now and would have to fend for myself if it wasn't for her.

I had to hand over most of my benefit to Mimi because she didn't get paid for me anymore. I gave it to her without argument because it was a real fear of mine that I would end up sleeping rough in shop doorways. That's what Mimi said would happen to me if I didn't have her to look after me and I believed her. I didn't care that she took most of my benefits because I didn't need very much to live on; my books were free from the library and watching television was free.

Every now and then Mimi would get disgruntled over something – this usually happened after one of her food phases had ended and she had yet to find her next obsession and she'd take it out on me. She'd lumber up the stairs and shout at me, tell me how I'd ruined her life. One time she threw my TV down the stairs because she hated that I got enjoyment from it but I saved up and got another from the second hand shop. I knew that her black mood wouldn't last forever and once she'd found a new food to fixate on we'd have peace for a while.

I never considered that I could have a life without her, it just didn't seem possible.

And then one day it did.

It was late, about ten-thirty in the evening, and I'd just finished watching the final part of a BBC thriller and had come downstairs to make myself a drink before I went to bed. As I got to the foot of the stairs I heard a strange noise coming from the lounge, a muffled thumping and flapping sound, and as I opened the lounge door I could see that it was Mimi making the noise. She looked almost comical; her feet in her pink fluffy slippers were slapping up and down on the carpet in front of her armchair and she was clutching her throat with her hands. I look back now and wonder if she was banging her feet to try and get my attention because she couldn't speak.

It was immediately obvious that she was choking. At the time she was going through her sherbet lemon boiled sweet phase and she must have inhaled one of them whole. She was obsessed with them and would suck and crunch them constantly, all day. It had got to the point that I had to go further afield to buy them as the local newsagents had sold out because she ate so many.

I went into the lounge and stood in front of her in shock and wondered what I should do. I had a vague idea that I needed to get behind her and wrap my arms around her middle and jerk upwards under her diaphragm to dislodge the sweet. To do that I would need to get her out of the chair which would be a task in itself because she was so huge. She was far bigger than me and I didn't know if I could do it on my own. But I knew that I would at least have to try although I wasn't sure if my arms would reach around her. I stood in front of her and tried to decide whether to attempt it before ringing for the ambulance or to just ring straightaway, because the sooner they got here, the better chance she would have.

Or maybe I should do neither.

Because it occurred to me as I stood watching her choke that it would solve a lot of problems if she died. I could have the house and I wouldn't have to put up with her any longer and my life would be far better without her in it.

The foot flapping increased in intensity and I looked at Mimi and she was staring at me, her face a strange purple colour, and I thought how very ugly she looked; how very ugly she'd always looked, actually. And then I stepped out into the hallway and pulled the lounge door closed and went back upstairs and sat on my bed for a while and read another couple of chapters of my book.

When I thought enough time had passed I went back downstairs and stood in the hallway and listened and the foot flapping had stopped.

I spent that night searching the house from top to bottom and by dawn I'd found nothing. I knew with certainty that Mimi had a lot of money hidden somewhere because the only things she ever spent money on beside the utility bills were the grocery shop and fish and chips. But try as I might, I could find nothing of any substance, just a few ten-pound notes and some loose change in her purse.

I found her latest bank statement and there was a balance of only a few hundred pounds and I could see that aside from her regular direct debits she drew out most of her money on her weekly trip to the bank.

At seven o'clock I knew that I couldn't delay calling for an ambulance any longer; my story was that I'd gone to bed last night and hadn't discovered her until this morning when I came down for breakfast. If I waited any longer it would look suspicious and I wasn't sure how I would cope if I was questioned too intently.

As it transpired, I needn't have worried because when the paramedics and on-call doctor arrived they expressed little surprise at Mimi's death; perhaps they see people choke to death every day.

They were very kind to me and were concerned at what a shock Mimi's death must have been for me and asked if there was anyone they could call. I probably did look sad; they never knew it wasn't because Mimi was dead but because I couldn't find her money and felt that I was going to go mad searching for it. I said no, that there was no one they could call and that I'd be okay. Then I surprised myself by asking if I could go to the hospital with Mimi. I have no idea why I said it and in hindsight can only think that I wanted to make quite sure that she was dead. Luckily, they said that I wasn't able to go with her but that I would have an opportunity to see her before the funeral.

I hadn't even thought of the funeral and had no clue what would be required of me but this was taken out of my hands by a woman from Social Services whom the NHS had contacted. My thicko act had worked extremely well with the ambulance crew and they had assumed that I would be unable to cope on my own. She arrived unannounced the day after Mimi was taken away and told me what I needed to do as if I could barely manage to wash and dress myself. She bought a prescription of sleeping tablets *to help me through it all* and I didn't even have to go to the chemist to get them because she'd already done so. She obviously didn't think I was capable. You wouldn't think that a doctor would be allowed to prescribe sleeping tablets for a patient he'd never met but things are different when you're on the register;

normal rules don't apply. I never took them but I still have them, because you never know.

Anyway, she took over everything to do with the funeral so I didn't have to do a thing and she also set in motion moving me from Mimi's council house into a one bedroom flat which would be easier for me to manage.

I didn't care what they did for the funeral because as far as I was concerned they could take Mimi to the local tip and chuck her in there. The social worker asked if I wanted a wake and I looked at her dumbly and asked what a wake was. Of course I knew what it was but she took me seriously and patiently explained it all to me. I wanted to laugh but I managed to look like I was listening and when she'd finished I said no, that I didn't think that I could get through it and she agreed with me so thankfully, it was the burial and then straight home. I was surprised to hear that Mimi had reserved herself a plot to be buried next to her parents; I'd always assumed that she'd been dragged up like me.

There were a few people at her funeral but I never spoke to them so I have no idea who they were; as far as I was aware Mimi had no friends and as for family, who knows? The social worker never mentioned if Mimi had made a will and I never found one on my search so I assume not; what little she left would have gone to the state if there were no blood relatives to leave it to. At best it would probably have amounted to a few hundred pounds so I didn't feel as if I was missing out. The social worker said that I was to take whatever furniture I wanted from the house to furnish my new flat, so I'm guessing anything that was left went to the council rubbish tip as it wasn't fit for anything else.

So I came home from the funeral and spent the rest of the day packing up my possessions to get ready to move into a flat which would, apparently, be more suitable for me. It wasn't too far away, the social worker assured me, so that I wouldn't be uprooted from my surroundings completely. She said this as if I had friends and knew people in the area; I didn't tell her otherwise as there seemed no point.

I didn't care about leaving the only home that I'd ever known as it meant nothing to me and I'd already started planning my new life; the life where I would be far away from a shitty one-bedroom flat and a run-down council estate.

A life where I would be a new person with a new life and have everything that I'd ever wanted. All I had to do was be patient and wait for my plan to come to fruition, which wasn't a problem because I'm good at waiting. So I was contented and felt almost jolly as I packed up my belongings.

Because, by then, I'd found Mimi's money.

CHAPTER ELEVEN

I've done a lot of thinking by the time I arrive for my shift on Tuesday night and I've made the decision that I'm going to tell Tash that she can't move in.

Quite honestly, I can't be doing with the stress of it; although it won't be too much longer until all the cash is paid into the accounts. I still have the safe in my wardrobe which Tash would be sure to notice and then there would be questions.

I would like us to be friends because she's fun and I haven't had much of that in my life but her moving in will just complicate things. Also, I only have one bedroom and I don't want to share a bed with her – I'm used to having my own personal space and it's all too much. Besides, once the cash is in the accounts there's nothing to keep me here any longer and I'll be moving on.

So I wasn't looking forward to my shift when I arrived at the back entrance to the chippy and was mentally rehearsing what I was going to say to Tash. The first thing that was odd was that Fred wasn't in his usual spot – sitting on an upturned bucket smoking a roll-up. He wasn't in the kitchen either and as I hung my bag up on the hook and put my overall on I could hear a terrific row coming from the shop; the sound of Fred shouting and someone, a woman, screaming at him. I looked at my watch to see that it was only five-fifteen; we don't open until five-thirty so it couldn't be a customer – which meant that it must be Tash or Stacey. I dithered for a few minutes – do I go and interrupt or stay in the kitchen out of the way until it's all over? In the end nosiness gets the better of me and I'm walking through to the front when Stacey barges past me, sobbing loudly with her eyes all red and puffy. She barely notices me as I slink back out of her way.

'You can stuff your fucking job,' she screams at Fred, who has followed her and is now standing in the doorway frowning at her, legs planted firmly apart and arms folded across his vast stomach.

'Keep your voice down or I'll call the police,' he booms at her. I've never heard Fred raise his voice before and I look at him in surprise.

'I haven't done nothing wrong, Fred,' Stacey shouts at him. 'Why don't you believe me? I've worked here for years, you know me, you know what I'm like and it weren't me.'

Fred shakes his head.

'I know and I'm sorry about that Stacey but the facts don't lie. I marked those fivers and you had all of 'em in your pocket. I thought you'd been at it for a while and I did warn you. You were the only one working here this lunchtime with me so who else could it be? Remember what I said last week, about nicking? That was for your benefit, to give you another chance to stop. I wouldn't have done that for anyone else but you still carried on doing it, so I can't have you here no more.'

I remember; last week he leaned up against the chip fryer and gave the three of us a little pep talk before we opened, about honesty and doing a good night's work. I didn't take much notice of what he was saying at the time because he quite often talks random shit at the start of each shift. With hindsight, it was obviously a warning to Stacey which she didn't heed.

'You're wrong.' Stacey rips her overall over her head and flings it onto the floor in front of Fred. 'It weren't me, I've been fitted up and you can't even see it.'

'Calm it down, Stacey.' Fred says evenly. 'No one's fitted you up and don't try and blame other people because you've been caught fair and square. If you were struggling for money you should have come to me, I'd have helped and given you more shifts but I can't have you thieving from me.'

'I weren't struggling and I don't need your fucking help.' Stacey storms past Fred towards the door and as she passes me she knocks into me so hard that I tumble backwards and crash into the wall, landing on my backside.

'You sure you're alright, mate?' Tash's big blue eyes look down at me with concern and I nod. I'm sitting on Fred's upturned bucket *getting my breath back* as Fred puts it. He insisted I sit here until I've recovered; I think he's frightened I'm going to make a claim for industrial injury or something. I'm actually fine – I've suffered far worse than being knocked into accidentally. I'm quite enjoying the attention though.

'I'm just in shock, I suppose,' I lie. 'I still can't believe Stacey was stealing because hadn't she worked here forever?'

'Yeah, she had, stupid cow, she had all the daytime shifts and everything so there'll be some extra going spare now.' Tash says. 'It was obvious it was her too because when she was off sick it didn't happen. Talk about thick as shit.'

Stacey was no Einstein but I didn't think she was so stupid as to make it so obvious that it was her. I'd never noticed her stealing money from the till and putting it into her pocket – not that I was looking. She must have done it when it was just her and Fred and he was out in the back kitchen.

'Take no notice of her trying to blame you for fitting her up,' Tash says, quietly. 'Fred would never believe her because he caught her bang to rights.'

I look at Tash in surprise.

'She's blaming me?' I ask. 'Why would she think it was me?'

'No, forget it mate, I got that wrong, of course she doesn't blame you,' Tash says, unconvincingly.

'Why did you say it then?' I ask.

Tash sighs.

'Me and my big mouth. Okay, she does think it was you but I didn't mean to tell you 'cos it serves no purpose.'

'But what would I gain by fitting her up?' I ask.

'Who knows?' Tash shrugs. 'She's mental, always has been. And I wasn't going to tell you this but now she's gone I might as well; she's had it in for you since she met you. I didn't want to tell you 'cos it isn't nice and I thought if we all went out together and she got to know you she might like you but it didn't work.'

I think back to my first shift with Stacey, she wasn't exactly friendly to me and never has been. I didn't think she liked me so it turns out I was right. Not that I'm bothered; I didn't like her anyway although it means that Fred will replace her and the new person probably won't like me either.

Tash looks around to make sure that Fred isn't in earshot and then leans closer.

'I think,' she whispers. 'That she was going to set you up and get you the sack but Fred caught her before she got the chance. If she hadn't had the marked notes on her I'd of been asked to turn out my pockets and so would you.'

I stare up at Tash.

'And if you think about what happened on Saturday night, it all makes sense,' Tash continues.

'What happened?' I still have no memory of Saturday night, no matter how hard I try to remember.

'You can't remember what she did to you?' Tash looks at me wide-eyed. 'None of it?'

'No, not a thing. I remember Stacey crying and getting chucked out of the club but that's it, it's a blank after that.'

Tash stands back and fold her arms.

'She's psycho, mate, a fucking psycho.' She looks over her shoulder, checking again for Fred but he's in the shop serving the first of the customers – he couldn't wait to leave me and Tash to it after Stacey left; I think he's had enough drama for one night.

'That's the reason she got chucked out – 'cos she went for you and said you were out to ruin her. Said you'd set her up with them blokes what were watching her dancing. They took her out to one of their cars and treated her like a slapper and she said it was all your fault.'

'What?' is all I can manage to say.

'Yeah, I know. Like I say, not right in the head.' Tash makes a circling motion round her head with her finger.

'But why? Why would I do that?

Tash shrugs. 'Fuck knows. But you're not

dealing with a rational person, are you? Stacey isn't right in the head, never has been. She was the same at school, always lying and nicking stuff just because she could. She got sent away you know, to one of those special schools, she was such a head case. Quite sad really.'

It is. Not quite as sad as my life in the top trumps game of life, but pretty sad.

'Quite lucky that Fred caught her when he did, 'cos who knows where it would have ended,' Tash says, thoughtfully.

'What d'you mean?' I ask, just as Fred bellows *you two coming or what?* from the front of the shop.

'Just,' Tash hesitates, biting her lip. 'Be careful, you know. Don't go down any dark alleys on your own.'

Fred bellows again.

'Coming!' Tash answers. And with that, we start our shift.

Over the rest of my shift, when the shop was quiet and Fred was on one of his many breaks, I got the rest of the story out of Tash. I'm in shock that Stacey thought I'd somehow engineered the group of lads leering at her on the dance floor. Apparently when she disappeared she was with them all in the car park and it turned into a bit of an orgy in the back of one of their cars. Tash said that Stacey was fine with that but the fact that they then told her to fuck off because *they didn't hang around with slags* was what upset her. I think Tash is right and she's off her head because what did she expect? She was the one jiggling her tits and arse in all their faces.

It did make me feel sick for her though; because she may be a slag but from what Tash said she *was* in a right state when she came into the club later and I do remember that, the state of her; dishevelled with her clothes all grubby and crying hysterically. I said as much to Tash; I even suggested that maybe I should track Stacey down and let her know that it wasn't me, that I definitely didn't set her up. Although as soon as I said it, I knew that I wouldn't do it, but it sounded good; it sounded like what a normal person would say. Tash warned me not to; she said that stealing wasn't the only reason that Stacey went to a 'special school'; she said she'd bottled another girl at a party when she was a teenager. She said she had a bottle in her hand on Saturday night so I was going to get the same treatment so the best thing I could do was stay well away from her. She said that she wrestled the bottle off Stacey and got the bouncers to throw her out and that sparked a memory in me; a flashback of Stacey and Tash fighting, Stacey's face red with rage whilst Tash appeared calm and almost amused.

Tash stopped Stacey from ramming a bottle into my face.

Tash didn't even seem bothered about it; in

fact she was surprised when I thanked her, she said it was only what she'd do for any mate. Which got me thinking; maybe I'm being a bit harsh not letting her move into my flat, maybe, it wouldn't be such a bad thing after all. Because realistically, there's nothing still keeping me here is there? There's actually nothing stopping me from moving away right now and starting my new life except for my fear, because I could have started my new life already and the only reason I haven't is because I'm afraid. I'm afraid that my new life will be exactly the same as the old one except that I'll have money.

I think I need to gain some confidence for this new life of mine; maybe if Tash moves in I can start to become the new person that I want to be and then once everything is in place, I'll move on. And at the same time I could do Tash a big favour, because once I'm gone she can have the flat to herself because unless she gets herself on the council waiting list she'll never get a place of her own – and even then it'll take years.

I've discovered tonight that Tash is my friend. She stuck up for me when she didn't have to, because as far as she's concerned, that's what friends do.

Tash can move in because apart from anything else, I owe her.

CHAPTER TWELVE

I get up early on Sunday morning because Tash is moving in this afternoon and I want to make sure that everything is ready for her. Now that I've had a good think about it I've come round to the idea and think it will be good for me in my transition to becoming a normal person.

I've cleaned the flat – although it was already clean because I'm not a messy person – and I've changed the sheets on the bed. We haven't discussed sleeping arrangements but there is only one bed so we'll have to share it unless Tash brings another one with her – which she would have to put in the hall as there is no room in the bedroom or lounge. Anyway, it's a big double bed so there's plenty of room and lots of people share beds and think nothing of it; I just need to get over my dislike of being close to people.

I've solved the problem of the safe – it's still in exactly the same place, in my wardrobe, but no one would know it was there unless they looked for it. On Thursday I measured the safe and then went down to the local hardware shop and got the old bloke in there to cut me five pieces of something called MDF. I told him I was making a storage box to put things in although I don't know why I felt I had to explain myself to him. He said MDF was cheaper than buying proper wood and will do the job. I didn't care what it is as long as it hides the safe. I don't think he charged me any extra for cutting it but I wouldn't have minded if he had because it saved me having to buy a saw. Also, I'd have had trouble getting a big piece of wood or MDF home. As it was I had a bit of a struggle and had to stop quite a few times for a rest because five pieces of MDF are very heavy. I bought some wood glue and paint from him as well and after lunch I spent the afternoon making a box to fit over the safe so it looks as if some pipes or something are boxed in. I got the idea from looking around the flat because there are similar boxed in bits all over it, mostly in the bathroom and kitchen. I painted the box with two coats of white emulsion and it doesn't stand out too badly; especially as once the paint was dry I stacked a pile of t-shirts on top of it and draped one down over the front. Then I stacked my shoes and trainers in front of it so it was even less noticeable.

I've shoved all of my clothes – which isn't many

– over to one side of the wardrobe so that Tash can have the other side for her stuff. I did the same with the chest of drawers so now I have the top two drawers and Tash can have the bottom two to put her things in.

The money from underneath the floorboards is gone now although there is still a fair bit in the safe. My mobile phone and my purse with my cards inside are also in there.

I've thought of a new place to store my things that's even more secure than the safe, but for the moment they're fine where they are. I don't like to do things in a panic; it's best to think stuff through and not rush into things as that's when mistakes happen.

I took all of the cash from underneath the floorboards when I went into town on Friday morning and I paid it into the accounts – nearly a thousand pounds in each one. One of the bank clerks gave me a bit of a surprised look but I just ignored her and wouldn't meet her eyes. I have to keep reminding myself that I don't need to explain myself to anyone, especially complete strangers. Mimi and Aaron are both dead and I'm a grown woman with a life of my own and I can do whatever I like. Even so I'll be glad when I've finished paying all the money in because it's become a bit of a chore.

Once I'm settled into my new life I need to seriously look into investments; now that I've got the majority of the cash into the system I need somewhere that will give me a good rate of return.

I have a post office account for my chip shop wages and I can live comfortably off that until I leave and the social still pay my rent because I earn so little. I just hope the nosy social worker doesn't decide to pay me a visit anytime soon because there'll be questions if she finds out I have someone else living with me. It'll cause a problem with my rent being paid so I want to avoid it if at all possible.

It's very unlikely the social worker will visit though; I'm not a priority anymore. I don't think that I ever was.

I haven't discussed rent with Tash but I'm not going to ask too much from her; just enough to cover half of the electric bill as the water rates and rates are included in my rent. And food; she'll have to pay for half of that too but all in all, she can live here pretty cheaply and I think I'm being very generous because most people would ask for more and want to make a bit of profit out of sharing their flat.

I've tried to make the place welcoming for Tash; I've plumped up the cushions on Mimi's old plum velour sofa and I even went into the seconds shop whilst I was in town and bought six wine glasses so we don't have to drink wine out of mugs anymore. They were only one-ninety-nine and I know that makes it look as if I intend drinking alcohol again but I don't, I'm just going to pretend to drink it because Tash will think I'm weird if I don't.

When I worked my shift last night it was just me and Tash as Fred hasn't replaced Stacey yet. It was very busy and we had to work extra hard but Fred's so tight, he never offered us a bonus or anything. All night Tash kept saying how she was really looking forward to moving in today and she said she'd packed everything up ready. She said her mum didn't mind too much although she said she'd miss Tash. The way she spoke about her it sounded like they're really close and I couldn't help feeling a bit jealous.

Tash never mentioned about going out last night like we did last Saturday and I wondered if she was going out with someone else. She says she hasn't got a boyfriend but she's always on her phone and she never accepts any offers when she gets chatted up, even from the good-looking ones. It's not any of my business because she doesn't have to tell me but if we're friends, which I think we are, then I hope she'll like me enough to confide in me and treat me like a proper mate.

Not that I'll be confiding in her; no way. *By the way, I'm a bit of a serial-killer* is a conversation stopper and there's no way anyone's going to want to be my friend if I tell them that.

Tash has picked up Stacey's lunch time shifts and Fred offered me some but I said no; I can manage on what I earn now and five nights a week is more than enough for me. Tash says no matter what she earns it's never enough.

One of the reasons I didn't want any more shifts is because when Tash is doing a lunchtime shift it'll give me a chance to get into my safe without fear of being caught and also have a bit of time on my own. I have definite plans for a different hiding place but as I said before, I don't like to be rushed when I make arrangements.

Tash.

That's an awful name, isn't it? Much too similar to moustache which no girl in her right mind wants to be associated with. Tash doesn't have even the faintest hint of a moustache but imagine if she did? Her mother clearly wasn't thinking when she named her. I assume Tash is short for Natasha but maybe it's not; maybe that's her actual name. I don't know why people insist on shortening perfectly good names and ruining them, I think it's a shame. If my name was Natasha I think I'd rather be called *Nat* and be thought of as an insect than a hairy top lip. My real name is Ellen but I actually prefer Ellie because it doesn't sound so old-fashioned. Aside from the *smelly Ellie* bit of course, but now I don't get called that because I don't see anyone that I used to be at school with. Or if I do see anyone, I make sure that they don't see *me*.

Mimi wasn't Mimi's name either, although I didn't find that out until after she'd died. When I saw the death certificate I thought they'd got the wrong person because the name on it was Muriel. Muriel. Can you imagine being lumbered with that? I can't say I blame her for changing it because who the hell is called Muriel nowadays? Even though Mimi was ancient, fifty-two according to her death certificate, there are limits. I don't know why she chose to call herself Mimi because it sounds vaguely French and there was nothing remotely French about Mimi. Although she did smell of onions because she didn't wash very often and they always show French people on the telly with a string of onions around their necks so maybe that was why.

I'm going for something a bit different in my new life; different but upmarket, because I don't want one of those new made-up names that all the chavy pop stars seem to go for. I'll stick to the old-fashioned names that all the well-to-do people use to name their kids because I can do a pretty good posh accent when I put my mind to it.

Quarter-to-one.

Tash will be here soon.

Everything is ready, now I just have to wait.

Tash didn't arrive until nearly three o'clock and I was beginning to think that she'd changed her mind about moving in. Whilst I was thinking this, I couldn't decide whether I was pleased about it or not. I'd just starting getting on my own nerves by over-thinking it all when the doorbell rang and she arrived.

I opened the front door and there she was with two giant suitcases; she said she'd got a mate to give her a lift in his car and she'd only bought clothes with her for now. I was annoyed with myself because if I hadn't been thinking about her changing her mind and whether I was pleased about it or not, I'd have seen who dropped her off because I'd been looking out of the window every five minutes before that. She said she still had more stuff to bring but would get it over the next few weeks. I hid my surprise because all of my clothes wouldn't even fill one suitcase, let alone two.

We struggled down the hall with them and I helped her unpack it all and put it away. By the time we'd finished my clothes were crammed into a quarter of the wardrobe and hers filled the rest. She couldn't fit all the other stuff in two drawers so she piled it up in the bottom of the wardrobe and put all of her shoes in the hall cupboard where I keep the vacuum cleaner. I don't really do clutter because I don't have that much stuff so aside from the vacuum the cupboard was almost empty. It's full now; Tash must have brought twenty pairs of shoes with her which she said is only half of what she owns. She did stack them in there neatly though, so I don't think it'll be a problem; I can live with that.

After we'd put everything away and put the suitcases underneath the bed, I made us a cup of tea and we sat in the kitchen. I really wanted to know who the mate was that had dropped her off in his car but couldn't think of a way of finding out without actually asking. I also wanted to know if she went out clubbing last night but ditto; I'm going to have to get over this wanting to know because it's not important, is it?

We sat and drank our tea and Tash chatted away like she does and then she asked if I had any biscuits and I said no – I never buy them, Mimi's custard cream phase put me off for life – and then Tash asked what we were going to have for tea tonight. I normally have a sandwich because I've lost my appetite for cooked food since I've been at the chippy. Even before that my cooking only consisted of egg on toast or scrambled eggs. Tash surprised me then by saying that she likes to cook. She said if I had the ingredients she'd cook us a lasagne for tea or a Spaghetti Bolognese. I realised then that the only food in the cupboards was bread, cereal and tins of beans and some butter and cheese in the fridge because that's what I live on. I felt a bit embarrassed because I thought I'd got everything ready and I never even thought about getting any food in.

So when we finished drinking our tea we went to the *Tesco's Local* just along the street from the chippy. I don't usually go there because it's quite expensive. I get most of my stuff from the Lidl or Aldi in town but as it was a Sunday all the big supermarkets shut early. I thought well, it can't hurt just to get a few things to keep us going until we can go shopping properly, even if it is a bit pricey.

Except we didn't just buy stuff for our tea; Tash took one of the little trollies that they have there and by the time we got to the till it was full up. As the checkout boy was ringing it up I was thinking this is going to be expensive and it was – fifty-four pounds and forty-six pence – and I could have bought twice that amount of stuff from Lidl for the same amount. Not that I ever spend that much; twenty quid usually does me.

So while me and Tash packed it into bags I'd worked out that it would be twenty-seven pounds and twenty-three pence each. Still more than my normal week's shop but it's not every day that your only friend in the world moves into your flat, is it? And then the bags were packed – four of them, not much for fifty odd quid – and Tash picked up one in each hand and the checkout boy looked at me and Tash looked at me and I realised.

I was the one that was going to be paying.

CHAPTER THIRTEEN

We're going out tonight after we've finished work; I'm going to wear the same outfit as I wore the last time because that's all I have although Tash has said I can borrow something of hers if I like. I don't think I will because no one's going to notice that I wore the same thing two weeks ago.

It's the first time since we went out last time that I'll be wearing something that isn't leggings and giant t-shirts because that's all I have. I'm not bothered about buying more; maybe if Tash suggests a shopping trip I will. Although I'll have to wait until I get paid because the shopping was an unexpected expense.

Fred still hasn't replaced Stacey and Tash says she doesn't think he's going to because we seem to be managing alright between the three of us. I think he's tight; the least he could do is give us a pay-rise to make up for the extra work but there's no sign that he's going to do so. He's going to be in the lurch when I leave to start my new life and it serves him right. Or what if me and Tash were both ill – what would he do then?

It's been strange living with someone else this last week; much better than I thought it would be – it's not like living with Mimi or Aaron at all so I won't have to murder Tash.

Only joking; I only murdered Aaron because I had to and strictly speaking, Mimi was an accidental death, at least that's what the coroner said.

Tash is like me, very neat and tidy and if she makes a mess in the kitchen she clears up after herself; likewise the bathroom. She's the perfect flatmate, even sleeping with her isn't a problem as she doesn't hog the bed and we sleep soundly without any parts of our bodies touching. She's a very good cook, too, although she's quite wasteful as she always cooks far too much but won't consider freezing it or eating it the next day. She says reheated food is bad for you and causes cancer.

Yes, everything has worked out well except for one thing.

The rent.

It hasn't been mentioned; Tash hasn't asked me how much I want and I haven't told her how much I expect her to pay. It's all a bit awkward and I know

I should just come straight out and ask her but I can't, in the same way that I couldn't ask her to pay for half of the shopping that we bought on Sunday. I just don't know how to say it yet I know that the longer I let it go on the harder it's going to be. I just need to ask her and get it over with but I keep putting it off.

The thing is, if I don't ask her soon I'm going to run out of money and then I'll have to go into town and draw some cash out of one of the accounts. The trouble is that we get on so well that I'm just going to feel petty saying it because she's offered me her clothes to wear and she says to help myself to any of her makeup and stuff. I'm going to feel like a tight arse mentioning money.

I also thought the food that we'd bought on Sunday would last all week but it didn't and we'd run out of teabags, milk, bread and butter by Wednesday. Tash can drink tea for England, she constantly has a cup on the go, God knows how she keeps her teeth so white. So when we ran out, I thought this is it, now I'll have to say something but Tash beat me to it; she said that she couldn't go to the shop because she was working a lunch-time shift but if I stocked up she'd give me the money when she got home. I felt relieved that I didn't have to ask her so I went and re-stocked. I bought some chocolate digestives because the three packets we'd bought had all gone – Tash has a very sweet tooth – and I thought when she's finished her shift and pays me for the food that'll be a good opportunity to bring up the subject of the rent.

Except that she didn't pay me; it wasn't mentioned at all and I couldn't find the right words to ask so I'd paid again; Eleven pounds and twenty-two pence. It's embarrassing and it's the only thing that's spoiling Tash moving in. I've had to go to the Post Office to draw some more cash out to go out with tonight and now there's hardly anything left in my account.

So I'm definitely going to ask her tonight.

We're going back to the flat to get changed after work and then we're going to the Solo Club again. I wasn't sure about going there in case Stacey is there because I don't want any trouble. Tash says not to worry because Stacey won't be there because she's heard that she's got a couple of black eyes and she's not going out until they've healed up. I asked Tash how she knew this and she said that a mate of hers who lives down the same street as Stacey, told her. Apparently Stacey just escaped being thrown out by her mum and dad when they found out she'd been sacked for thieving. Tash thinks that it might have been her dad who gave her the black eyes.

So I was relieved that Stacey wouldn't be at the Solo Club but I also felt a bit sick for her because I know what it's like to be knocked about. Then I reminded myself that Stacey tried to set me up and bottle me and I didn't feel sad for her anymore.

So, tonight's the night.

Time to talk about money.

I have a crick in my neck that brings tears to my eyes as I wake up and the vilest taste possible in my mouth. For a moment I seriously wonder if I've been eating shit. I open my eyes to the unfamiliar sight of plum velour and a bucketful of vomit.

The plum velour is the sofa, which I've slept on and the crick in my neck is due to the fact that I've somehow managed to sleep with my head hanging over the edge of the seat cushion. The bucket of vomit is in front of me on the floor and I assume the vomit is from me. My stomach rolls and I hastily close my eyes so I don't have to look at it anymore. I have no recollection of coming home or falling asleep on the sofa and I wonder what the hell I drank that would make me so drunk that I couldn't make it into bed.

Tash and I went to the Solo Club after sharing a bottle of wine here first, but I only drank one glass, I'm sure I did. I definitely remember arriving at the club; it was packed when we got there so I think it was late already, later than the last time we went. I remember dancing and laughing and having a great time but no specific events and like before, I don't remember getting home.

This is it; I obviously have zero tolerance for alcohol and from now on I won't be drinking any, even if Tash does think that I'm weird. I lie back and wait for my stomach to stop churning and am considering trying to haul myself from the sofa when I hear the unmistakable sound of a man's laughter coming from the bedroom down the hall.

My bedroom.

Tash has a man in there, in my bed, whilst I'm out here on the sofa, like the lodger. Try as I might, I cannot remember coming back here last night so have no idea who the man is. Is he Tash's boyfriend? The one that she says she doesn't have? He could be a casual one night stand which is worse, to me, because who knows what he's like – he could be an axe murderer or worse. I may be an almost serial killer but I only kill people when I have to; I'm quite safe otherwise. If she met him last night she will only have known him for a few hours and have no idea what he's really like. What if he's a thief and he finds the safe and manages to break it open? I feel panic starting to rise and I'm hauling myself off the sofa, head spinning and stomach churning, when I hear the front door slam.

'Ooh, shit, you look dog rough.' Tash appears in the lounge doorway, her Primark satin dressing-gown pulled around her.

I look at her through bleary eyes and flop back down onto the sofa.

'Who was that? I manage to mutter.

Tash bites her bottom lip, her face full of guilt.

'Oops, sorry about that. An old mate.'

I stare at her.

'I'll change the bed, of course,' she says. 'I didn't mean for it to happen, sorry. I drank far too much.'

She doesn't look like she drank too much, she looks like she's had a good eight hours sleep on her own and looks disgustingly bright-eyed and bushy-tailed.

'A mate?' I say.

'Yeah, a mate with benefits. I only hook up with him when I've had too much. And he was absolutely wasted; Christ knows how he even managed it. I think he did though I really can't really remember.' She laughs.

'I don't feel comfortable about it,' I say, surprising myself.

'Don't you?' Tash says, in surprise. 'Because you weren't bothered last night, you insisted on taking the sofa so we could have the bed. You told us to go and have fun.'

'Did I?'

'Yeah, you said I should enjoy myself and you'd keep out of the way and that I could do the same for you sometime.'

I lay my head on the back of the sofa and wait for the queasiness in my stomach to settle before I answer.

'Well,' I say, with what I hope is firmness. 'I'm honestly not comfortable with it so it must have been the drink talking.'

'Okay, no problem,' Tash says, with a shrug. 'Do you want a cup of tea?'

I clamp my hand over my mouth but it's no

good, the mention of tea is too much and I lean forward, pull the bucket towards me and vomit into it. It's disgusting and there's gallons of it spewing from my mouth. The sight of it makes me vomit even more until I'm sure there can be nothing left in my stomach. When I've finished dry heaving I lean back against the sofa and close my eyes and feel the bucket being taken from my hands. I open my eyes to see Tash carrying it with her towards the door.

'Thanks,' I say, in a pathetic voice.

'No problem, what are friends for, eh?'

As she's about to go I decide that now is the moment, the moment to ask about the rent. I feel like I've just died but I need to get it over and done with because if I don't say it now, I never will.

'Tash?' I say.

'Yeah?' she asks, stopping by the doorway.

'The rent,' I say. 'I've been meaning to say to you about it because we haven't agreed an amount, have we?'

'No, we haven't,' she says.

'I was thinking fifty quid a week?' I suggest. 'Paid in advance? And split the food bills down the middle?' This is more than I was going to ask for but I need to recoup some of what I've spent. Although fifty quid is still dirt cheap for somewhere to live.

'Sure,' she says with a smile. 'No problem.'

Despite feeling so ill I feel relief flood through me, I wasn't expecting it to be this easy. There was me, making a huge deal out of it and all I had to do was ask her. Why didn't I ask her before? She's my friend, she's not going to be offended. I feel mean now for making such a big fuss over her having her shag-buddy to stay over.

'But,' Tash says as she walks towards the door. 'Can you wait until I get paid on Friday? 'Cos I'm a bit short this week.'

CHAPTER
FOURTEEN

Am I a suspicious person? I never used to be but I think I'm becoming one. Take Tash, for instance; it's been over two weeks since I asked her to pay me rent.

I'm still waiting.

I did ask her again, after a week, and she launched into this great long story about having a big mobile phone bill to pay and how she'd lent one of her mates money and she was still waiting for them to pay it back. Only she never said 'lent' she said she 'borrowed her some money' but I knew what she meant because loads of people around here get it mixed up. I didn't correct her because I didn't want to look like a smart arse and also, even though she's my friend she still talks to me sometimes like *I'm* the thick one. She said her mate was supposed to pay it back last week but they didn't and Tash said how she's too generous for her own good sometimes. She went on and on and on and in the end I just wanted her to *shut the fuck up*. She said that as soon as her mate paid her what she owed – which was going to be the next day – she would pay me everything plus the following week's rent in advance. So I waited and what happened next day?

Nothing. Nada. Zilch.

So now I'm thinking, is she taking the piss out of me? Is she just using me so she can live in my flat for free and she's not really my friend at all? I really don't know, because we get on so well apart from the money side of things and she is fun, even watching telly with her is fun and she thinks of things to do that I wouldn't dream of. Although we haven't had any parties yet, which I'm pleased about.

Take the other night for instance; it was a Monday night so we weren't working and I was gearing myself up to ask her about the money again when she suddenly jumps up off the sofa and goes out to the kitchen and says I have to go and see what she's doing. So I followed her out and there she was, pulling egg-shells out of the swing bin. They were the shells from the egg on toast that we'd had for tea because that's all the food there was left and I was refusing to buy any more. Tash never made any comment about there being nothing decent to eat because I think she knew I wasn't going to get caught out again. She just made our tea with what there was – two eggs and the rest of a loaf of a bread. She had to slice the crust in two to make it enough, but anyway, there she was with the egg-shells in her hand and she grinned at me and put them into a bowl and started grinding them up with a spoon.

'I'm doing us a pamper evening,' she said.

And she ground those egg shells until they were powder and then she went into the bedroom and got her makeup case, which is the size of a small suitcase, and rooted around and found some sort of oil stuff and put a few drops in with the egg shells and mixed it up. Then she made me sit down on a kitchen chair and she started slapping it all over my face. It was a face mask, she said, which would make our skin lovely and soft and keep us young looking. I started laughing and she told me not to because then it wouldn't work; I had to keep my face still so it didn't crack. She did mine and then she put the rest of it on her face and I still hadn't asked her about the money and I couldn't while we had the face mask on because we weren't allowed to talk. We rinsed them off after ten minutes even though you were supposed to leave them on for twenty because they'd started to itch. I couldn't see any difference at all.

Then Tash got all her nail varnishes out and gave me a manicure and a pedicure. So I never asked her about the rent because it would have felt mean and ungrateful, considering all she was doing and also it was fun and I didn't want to spoil the fun. But most of all, to do the pedicure she had to touch my feet which I think is pretty amazing, because there's no way I'd touch anyone else's feet ever again. Mimi made me cut her toe-nails for her when she got too fat to bend over and I can tell you I used to gag. They were more like hooves than feet and actually, I think it's a form of child-abuse making your foster child cut your toe-nails. It should be made an actual crime.

Anyway, this is how it goes; I get suspicious and I gear myself up to ask her but somehow she seems to know and does something so that I don't feel I can ask her and then I'm back to square one. There's no food in the house at all now and we've been getting our tea at the chippy because we've been working. I haven't eaten much because after a couple of chips I've had enough, especially when I think how dirty Fred is and how he's touched it all. I try to convince myself that cooking it destroys Fred's germs but it doesn't always work. I prefer to have a fish cake or a sausage if I can but we have to be a bit careful because Fred notices; I think he counts them.

I need to stop calling it 'tea' as well because that's a very working class turn of phrase. It's dinner, not tea, and dinner, eaten at midday is actually lunch because it's not a main meal like it was at school when we called it dinner time. Very confusing, but it won't matter how posh I sound if I still refer to dinner as 'tea;' It'll stand out a mile that I'm an imposter.

So I'm in a dilemma about Tash, part of me wants her to go and the other doesn't. I wish she'd just pay the rent and then I wouldn't have to think about it. There are also a few things that are starting to niggle at my brain and if she just paid up I wouldn't be thinking like it; I'd be enjoying living with a friend who is fun and enjoying myself like a normal twenty-one year-old should.

Sometimes I feel like just clearing off now and starting my new life without even telling her and then she can have the flat to herself and I won't have to be thinking that she's not my friend at all and she's just using me.

But I'm not; I'm going to work instead.

It was the usual Saturday night at the chippy; run off our feet and Fred getting sweatier and sweatier with each batch of chips he cooked. Even with the fans blowing he still stank the place out. I don't think it'll be any different in the winter either because he's one of life's sweaters. I've come across his type before, no matter what they do they're dripping in perspiration. Mimi wasn't a sweater but she never actually did anything so maybe that's why. Perhaps if she'd been set to work in a chip shop she'd have sweat like a pig, too.

I waited all night to see if Tash was going to mention going out tonight and my going out clothes were hanging in the wardrobe, washed and pressed so they were ready to wear. I thought she might suggest it because we never went out last Saturday – at least, I didn't. We walked home after our shift and I thought we were going to just watch telly but once we got in she vanished into the bedroom and came out all tarted up after about fifteen minutes. She said she was going round to see a mate who was going through a rough time and needed a shoulder to cry on. What could I say? I didn't believe her because she looked like she was dressed up to go out clubbing to me.

And that pissed me off, I won't deny it. Because she still hadn't paid any rent but clearly had money to go out clubbing – although she never pays to get in so it doesn't cost her that much, but still. Also, why didn't she ask me to go with her? Is it because I made a fuss about her 'mate' staying over in my bed? She didn't seem that bothered when I said I didn't like it but maybe she is and she's not going to ask me to go clubbing anymore.

I was prepared to give her the benefit of the doubt last week but tonight she didn't even walk home with me; as soon as we finished our shift she ran out the back door of the chippy and said she'd see me later. By the time I got outside she'd gone and all I could see were the tail lights of a car disappearing round the end of the alleyway.

I stomped home in a right old mood; who are all these 'mates' she keeps referring to? None of them seem to have names and I haven't met any of them and if you're friends with someone wouldn't you introduce them to your mates? I would if I had any. Which makes me think that she's ashamed of me or she's just using me, or both.

So, here I am again on my own and I'm thinking if she's not going to pay rent and go out with me what's the point of her living here? Okay, she's fun when she's here but if she's just 'being fun' to use me I'd rather she didn't bother.

And there are other things that are bothering me, which I've been trying to tell myself are coincidences but I don't think that they are. Somehow, she seems to know stuff about me that I'm sure I haven't told her. For instance, she said she'd had her name down for a flat for ages but has no hope of getting one because unlike me she's not *on the register.* I never told her anything about my past because she never actually asked and if she had asked, I'd have lied because no one needs to know about my shitty life. Another thing she said was that she'd never been to a funeral and what was it like? I said I didn't know and she said of course I wouldn't, but did I know of anyone who had? I think I caught her out but she thinks I didn't notice because she's under the illusion that I'm a bit thick and she's clever. There have been lots of little things that I probably wouldn't have thought anything of if it wasn't for the rent thing and her not going out clubbing with me anymore.

And it's made me feel fed up and it's made me do something that I wouldn't have done if she'd just paid the fucking rent and treated me like a friend.

I've set a trap.

Apart from thinking that she knows stuff about me, I've had the definite feeling that she's been going through my stuff. I'm very particular about my things and everything I have is in its proper place and if it's not, I notice. Other people wouldn't notice, but I do. My underwear drawer is precise, I line my knickers up with the edge of the flower on the wrapping paper that I've lined the drawer with and my bras are exactly on the fourth leaf down. Slightly OCD, I'll agree, but it's very helpful when you want to know if someone has been snooping through your stuff and I'm pretty sure that Tash has.

My knickers were only very slightly out of place but I noticed; also, the pile of t-shirts that I placed on the box over the safe are arranged in a particular order. The white t-shirt hanging down over the front of the box may look very casual but I know that it is exactly two centimetres from the edge of the box because I measured it with a tape measure. When I checked yesterday it was three centimetres from the edge so I knew that Tash had moved it because I certainly hadn't.

So I decided to set a trap; when Tash was out doing her lunch-time shift, I placed a piece of cotton thread from the bottom of the box to the edge of the floor in the wardrobe. It's not visible unless you actually look for it and I practised taking the box off the safe and each time the cotton thread came away.

When Tash came back after her shift I made a big deal of saying to her that I was going to have a long soak in the bath because I had a headache. This was so she'd know that she had plenty of time to snoop in safety. I ran a bath and stayed in there for a good hour and had the radio on too so that she didn't need worry about me hearing her. I was like a prune by the time I got out of that water.

So; all I need to do is check that the thread is still there. I want it to still be there because if it's not, then it'll prove that Tash has been looking through my stuff.

I go into the bedroom and open the wardrobe doors and crouch down in front of the wooden box that covers the safe and scrutinise it. As I suspected, the thread is missing which can only mean one thing.

Tash has been looking and she knows that I have a safe.

CHAPTER FIFTEEN

When it was getting closer to me moving out of Mimi's house and into the flat, the social worker took me to a place where I could pick out furniture for free. I never knew that such places existed; shopping without paying that didn't include stealing, my classmates at school would have loved it. The furniture wasn't new, obviously, it was donated by kind-hearted people who thought it would be easier to donate it to charity rather than pay for a skip to throw it all into.

I'm being unkind; some of it wasn't bad and even if it was hideous it was clean because the charity wouldn't accept dirty stuff. It wasn't just for the likes of me, ex-prisoners could get stuff from there and people from other countries who'd arrived here with absolutely nothing could furnish their entire house from it. The social worker said I was to pick whatever I wanted and she'd arrange to have it delivered to my flat ready for when I moved in. She said of course I was welcome to take whatever I wanted from the house – very generous, considering it wasn't hers – but I had to bear in mind that a lot of furniture in the house was very big, whereas my new flat would be very small. What she meant was that the stuff in Mimi's house was fit for the dustbin; even the mattress on my bed was so old and lumpy that I'd have been better off sleeping on the floor.

So I picked out a double bed for myself – a basic new mattress was supplied as second-hand ones weren't deemed hygienic – a small kitchen table and chairs, a chest of drawers, a coffee table for the lounge and a cooker, washing machine and fridge with a freezer box. I didn't want a lot as I don't like clutter. I also didn't intend staying in the flat for very long so there was no the point of getting loads of stuff that I'd have to dust and keep clean.

The social worker kept showing me the sofas and chairs because she said that Mimi's plum velour three piece suite would be far too big for my flat and that with that in the lounge I'd have room for little else. I said I didn't care, that the only other thing I needed in there was a coffee table and a television so that was fine. She shut up eventually because she said that the suite obviously had sentimental value and that was allowed, apparently. If I changed my mind and wanted something smaller it might be difficult to 'swing it' once I'd actually moved in, she told me. I think this was some sort of veiled threat to make me change my mind so I put on my dumb look and refused to talk about it. That did the trick and she dropped the subject. We then left the furniture depository and went back to Mimi's house where she filled in a mountain of paperwork that I had to sign. I took ages reading through each form, although I wasn't actually reading it I was just pretending to so I could enjoy the look of impatience on the social worker's face. I kept asking stupid questions which she had to answer and I could tell that she was itching to get away and I thought, you can wait, earn your salary and explain it all to me even though I'm not actually interested at all. I think that by the time she left the house she hated me in the way that most people do.

But I didn't care.

I enjoyed it.

The actual day of moving into my flat was the most stressful thing about Mimi dying; even more stressful than lying about when she died. I'd have much preferred to stay in Mimi's house; not because I liked it but because then I wouldn't have had the anxiety about all of the money. The new furniture that I'd picked out was already in the flat so all that needed moving was my clothes, personal possessions – which didn't amount to very much, the television and the three piece suite.

It would have been much easier if I had left the suite and the television and just taken my own few things because then the council wouldn't have needed to send a van and the two men that came with it wouldn't have had to struggle to get the three piece suite into the van. They weren't happy about it; they said it weighed an absolute ton and was really a three man job and not two. They were after a tip, obviously, even though they were being paid a wage by the council for doing a house move that consisted of a three piece suite and a few bits and bobs.

I ignored their whinging and concentrated on making sure that they didn't damage the sofa and chairs whilst moving them. It was an unbelievable relief when we arrived and they'd finally managed to get it up the three flights of stairs and into my flat. Much to their dismay, it wouldn't fit in the lift as it was far too big. There was also a sticky moment where they didn't think that it would fit down the hallway and into the lounge. I think they deliberately made a meal out of moving it in the hope of getting a tip but their histrionics were wasted on me and I closed the door on their miserable faces with relief.

It's true that the sofa and two armchairs pretty much fill the lounge. I wedged the coffee table in front of the sofa and the television underneath the window which left just enough space to walk between the sofa and chairs. It didn't take long to sort my few possessions out and tidy everything away and I decided when I finally sat down that now that the trauma of moving was over, I was glad to be somewhere new. The flat was shabby and there was damp in the bathroom but it was no worse than the condition of Mimi's house and at least the walls didn't echo with the memories of my miserable childhood.

I planned to go into town the following day and open up some savings accounts at different banks; I'd looked online at what I needed to take and I had my birth certificate, my new rent book for the flat to prove my address and several letters from social services vouching for me. I was hoping that the fact I'd just moved into the flat wouldn't be a problem. I couldn't see that it would because I'd be paying money in, not asking for a loan. As it turned out it wasn't a problem at all, just very time-consuming and tedious.

It felt strange looking at my birth certificate and seeing the names written in the mother and father section. Of course I know their names off by heart because they're imprinted on my brain. I have my mother's surname and not my father's, so I wonder if they were even together or if I was the result of a one night stand. I suppose I'm lucky that I have a father's name on there at all. One day, I'll look into it and maybe track one, or both of them down but for now, I'm not interested as I have other things to do.

My plan was to open as many accounts as possible and deposit the cash in them and make regular payments every week until all of the money was safely deposited. It would take quite a long time to deposit it all but it was all part of the plan.

I rooted around in my bag and pulled out the small hammer and the large tin of upholstery nails that I'd brought with me. I then pulled the sofa away from the wall slightly – no mean feat as it weighs a ton – and squeezed along behind it and squatted down by the corner of the sofa which is furthest from the door. Using the pointy bit of the claw hammer, I eased out the upholstery nails that held the back material of the sofa in place. When I'd pulled out enough to get my hand through, I inserted my hand into the back of the sofa and pulled out three wads of twenty and fifty-pound notes. The wads were approximately an inch thick and could contain anything from five hundred to a thousand pounds. I laid the notes on the floor and then carefully repositioned the velour and re-tacked it to the back of the sofa with new upholstery nails. I then picked the wads of notes up and inched back along the sofa, stood up and pushed the sofa back tight against the wall.

Perfect, no one would ever know.

As I never knew until the day that Mimi was buried.

I came back to the house after the funeral and

slumped in the armchair that Mimi always sat in and felt the worst that I'd ever felt in my life. Not because Mimi was dead or because I had to leave the house but because I knew that even though I was free of Mimi, my life would continue in exactly the same way as before. A life of no money on a shitty council estate with no prospect of ever having any sort of decent life. The beacon of hope that had sent out a glimmer of light when Mimi died was now extinguished because of my fruitless attempts to find her money. I'd searched the house from top to bottom – including the loft and the garden and even under and inside her mattress – and I still hadn't found a thing. Just what had Mimi done with all of the cash that she withdrew from the bank every week? She didn't spend it because she was very mean with the shopping and I had to account for every penny that I'd spent and we always had to have the supermarket value brands of everything. She couldn't have hidden it somewhere else because she never *went* anywhere. I'd followed her many times on her bank trips and it was always the same; straight to the bank and then onto the bus and straight home again.

It had to be somewhere.

And as I sat there in my misery and finally gave up on my dream, it came to me.

Where was the place that Mimi spent all of her time?

The armchair.

It was the work of minutes to pull out the

upholstery nails on the back of the armchair to discover that I was right. There it was, neatly stacked, wads and wads of notes, too many piles of cash to count. I pulled out a wad and counted the twenties and fifties and there was five hundred pounds in that first wad. I didn't count all of the other wads piled in there but I assumed they would all be similar amounts and as I pulled the material down and peered upwards into the chair I could see that the wads of notes filled the entire back. I counted them several times before I believed what I was seeing; there were a hundred and seventeen wads of notes.

I stared at the chair in disbelief and mentally calculated that if there was five hundred pounds in each wad then that would amount to over fifty-eight thousand pounds.

More money than I ever dreamed of.

I later discovered that five hundred in a wad was the smallest amount; sometimes there was as much as a thousand but mostly they averaged eight-hundred pounds.

Whilst I knew Mimi had money, I'd never imagined it would be this much; this money would be more than enough to begin my new life and get away from this horrible place. I could go somewhere new and get a job and be a completely different person.

But that was before I found that the sofa and other armchair were also stuffed full of money and I realised that getting a job wasn't a priority for a very long time.

Mimi had been, quite literally, sitting on a fortune.

CHAPTER SIXTEEN

I'm going to ask Tash to leave.

What's the point of having her living with me if she won't pay her way and I can't trust her?

No point at all.

I was all set to tell her yesterday but she never came home after her night out and I was like a cat on hot bricks all day waiting for her to return. I guessed that she'd stayed at one of her many mates' houses after she went clubbing but by the time I went to bed at eleven o'clock last night she still wasn't back. I think she's just using me and this made me more sure that I'm that I'm doing the right thing by telling her to move out. If she was a true friend she wouldn't ignore me, would she? Even so, I'd like to stay friendly with her because she's the only one that I have but realistically, I don't think that's going to happen.

I can live with not being friends because I'm used to it. It was nice while it lasted. I think I'm better off on my own for now. I might be lonely but I'm used to it; I've been alone for all of my life.

I don't know what actual time it was when she eventually came home but it seemed as if I'd been asleep for a long time when I felt her slide into the bed next to me. I wasn't about to have the *moving out* conversation with her then but I decided that as soon as she got up in the morning I was going to tell her. I've been up since eight o'clock and it's now half-past eleven and she's still lying in bed and I wish she'd just get up so I could get it over with. I don't feel bad about telling her to move out because it's her own fault. If she'd just paid her rent and not made me buy all of the food I wouldn't have noticed she'd been snooping and then I wouldn't have had to set a trap for her and everything would have been great. Anyway, it's not as if she has nowhere else to go; she can move back into her mum's.

I know that I don't actually need the money but that's not the point; Tash doesn't know that. As far as she knows I have less money than her as I work fewer shifts so why does she think that I can pay for her to live here? No, it's not right and she'll have to go. I've been running through my head how I'm going to say it and have come to the conclusion that I just have to spit it out and not try to sugar-coat it. It's not like when I asked Aaron to move out; Tash may be tight-fisted but she's hardly going to beat me up.

The sound of the bathroom door closing alerts me to the fact that Tash is awake and out of bed. I get up and walk quietly down the hall and stand outside the bathroom door. I can hear the sound of the shower flowing so going by Tash's normal routine, she'll be dressed and out here in about fifteen minutes.

I spend the next fifteen minutes wandering aimlessly around. I go into the bedroom and make the bed that Tash has just got out of and then go into the kitchen and put the kettle on to make us both a cup of tea. There is no milk so it'll be black. I'll make it after I've told her to leave so it won't look as if I'm bearing a grudge. At least when she's gone I can go and buy some food and not have to eat my tea at the chippy every night.

Dinner, I mean.

When Tash eventually saunters into the lounge she's wearing a brightly coloured shorts suit and a pair of strappy wedges with a white headband. She looks as if she's dressed to go out again and I put down the magazine I'm pretending to read and decide to come straight out with it before she disappears again.

'Hi, mate, how's it going?' she chirrups, all smiles.

'Good, ta,' I say. 'Look, I'm just going to come out and say this because there's no point in beating about the bush. I'm sorry, but it's not working out.'

Tash stares at me, a blank expression on her face.

'Us living together,' I add.

Tash doesn't even look surprised. She nods her head slowly.

'Yeah, you're right mate, I was going to say the exact same thing myself,' she says. 'Shame, 'cos bits of it was fun, but no, it's not really working, is it?'

So she must have known this was coming and is trying to save face. She's taking it really well and I decide to let her off the rent that she already owes me; not that I think there's a chance in hell of her actually paying it but I was going to ask so I don't look like a complete pushover.

'Yeah, we did have fun,' I agree. 'And you're alright about it, are you? I mean, we can still be friends, can't we?'

'Of course we can, mate. We're not going to fall out over something like this, are we?'

'No,' I say. 'We're not.'

'Great,' Tash says, with a smile. 'So, the question is, I suppose, when are you moving out?'

I stare at her and wonder if I'm hearing things. This is turning into a replay of my conversation with Aaron, but this time I'll be winning the argument.

'What?' I say, with a laugh. 'I'm not moving out, this is *my* flat, remember.'

'But I thought you said it's not working out, us living together,' Tash says, with a frown.

Is she really that thick? She's not, I know she's not, but she obviously thinks I am.

'I'm not going anywhere, Tash.' I say, calmly. 'This is my flat and the rent book is in my name. I let you move in to share the bills but now I'm asking you to move out.'

Tash doesn't speak.

'I'm sure your mum will be happy to have you back, you said she was going to miss you and didn't really want you to go. You don't have to move out straightaway; tomorrow will be fine.'

'You must be joking,' Tash snorts. 'No way am I moving back in with that old bag. No chance.'

'Okay Tash,' I say. 'It's up to you where you go but you can't stay here, it's not working and you haven't even paid any rent. I can't afford to pay for you to live here as well as me. I'm sorry, but you'll have to go.'

Tash starts to laugh then, I mean really laugh, like I've just told her the funniest joke in the entire world. She laughs so much that she has to wipe tears from her eyes when she eventually stops. I sit stony-faced and watch her and wonder what it is about me that makes people think that they can walk all over me.

I know what it is; I'm a natural victim and people assume that I'm stupid.

'Sorry,' she says, giving her eyes another wipe. 'But you do make me laugh. The thing is, Ellie, I'm not going anywhere. If you really insist on staying, I suppose you can, although you'll have to move out of the bedroom.'

I gawp at her, unable to believe what I'm hearing, wondering how she has the absolute nerve to say these things.

'You can have the sofa,' Tash adds.

'The sofa,' I repeat, robot-like.

'Yeah, 'cos me and my boyfriend are going to have the bedroom and you know the saying, two's company, three's a crowd. I mean, obvs he's up for a threesome but he's a bit fussy if you know what I mean.'

This causes even more laughing and I think if she carries on I might hit her.

'You said you never had a boyfriend,' I say, as if it matters.

'Of course I've got a boyfriend,' she snorts. 'What sort of sad arse do you think I am? Did you really think I was like you? We've been together for months and now he can move in here with me. Perfect, isn't it?'

I stand up from the sofa because I've decided that I am going to hit her, even if it's just a slap around the face, because I'm sure I'll feel the better for it. I'm not a violent person because Mimi and Aaron have put me off for life, but on this occasion I'm going to make an exception because I think it might be therapeutic.

I step towards her and the doorbell shrills loudly. Tash spins around before I get to her and practically races down the hall to the front door.

'That'll be him now,' she calls over her shoulder. 'He's bringing his stuff round.'

I stand and watch as Tash opens the front door but I can't see who's there because she flings her arms around whoever is outside and they embrace. After what seems like several hours of disgusting slobbering noises they finally release their grip on each other and come up for air. Tash comes back into the hall and the figure steps inside and closes the front door. I stare at him and wonder how I could have been so stupid as to think that Tash was my friend.

'Hi, Ellie,' says Oobie. 'Or should I say Jess?'

CHAPTER SEVENTEEN

The moment I saw Oobie, everything fell into place and I knew exactly why he was here. I remembered the chance meeting with him in the Solo Club where he pretended not to know who I am – that meeting was obviously engineered by him. The day that I met Tash to go shopping and glimpsed the edge of the mysterious man she was talking to outside Primark –that man was Oobie.

I can see now that Tash becoming my friend had been planned right from the moment she told Oobie about the new girl in the chip shop and he realised it was me. Now that I think back, on my first shift at the chippy, Tash was polite to me but that was all; polite. On the second night she was the nicest person that I'd ever met – because Oobie had already hatched his plan and Tash needed to befriend me so that she could move into my flat. Oobie's tried to get in here before; I let him in the first time he turned up but after that I didn't because I didn't trust him and I couldn't take the chance that he'd find my money and take it for himself.

He turned up at the door numerous times over a few weeks, banging on the door knocker for ages and eventually giving up when I wouldn't answer the door. I never get visitors and when he called round and I saw who it was through the spy hole, there was no way I was letting him in. I never made a noise to make him think that I was in but I think he knew I was. When he stopped coming round I thought he'd given up but I was wrong; he was just looking for another way in. Luckily for me, although this flat is shabby and old, the front door is solid. Short of breaking it down with a battering ram there's no way Oobie could have forced his way in without announcing his arrival to the world. I know what he wants; what he's always wanted – Aaron's stash of drugs and cash.

'Nothing to say Ellie?' Oobie asks as he drags a large holdall along the hall and through into the bedroom.

My bedroom.

'You can't just barge in here like that,' I say, as he pushes past me.

'Is that right?' he calls from the bedroom. 'Cos it looks like I just have.'

Tash saunters after him with a smirk on her face

and I follow behind her. I stand in the bedroom doorway and watch the pair of them. Oobie walks over to the wardrobe and yanks both doors open before dropping down onto the floor into a crouch. He grabs hold of the corners of the wooden box that I made and lifts it up to reveal the safe. As he takes the box off he chucks it behind him, sending all of my t-shirts scattering across the floor in the process. He gets down on his knees and leans into the wardrobe.

'So, Ellie,' he says in a conversational tone as he studies the safe. 'You've brought yourself a safe.'

I say nothing and fold my arms.

'Want to give me the number now so I can open it? Save yourself a load of grief?' Oobie says, turning his head to look at me.

'I don't know it,' I say. 'It was Aaron's and he never told me.'

Oobie sighs theatrically, stands up and walks over to me.

'Just fucking tell me the number,' he says. 'Aaron never had a safe 'cos if he had he wouldn't have kept his stash under the fucking bath. AND he would have told me because we were mates and he told me everything.'

'He only just got it,' I say. 'He put it in the day he died so he probably never got a chance to tell you.'

'Did he?' Oobie asks.

'Yes. He said he didn't think behind the bath panel was very safe.'

Oobie hesitates and for a moment I wonder if

he's going to believe my lie but then he laughs.

'You're not even a good liar. Aaron said you were as thick as shit so I have to say you've surprised me, I didn't think you had it in you but it's no good, you're not keeping it because it's mine. I. WANT. THE. NUMBER,' he shouts into my face. 'NOW. Is that simple enough for you to understand?'

I shrug and Oobie mutters *for fuck's sake* and turns to Tash.

'She must have someone else dealing for her,' Oobie says to her. ''Cos I can't see she's got the brains to do something like this on her own. Aaron said she was practically retarded and yet here she is with a fucking safe in the wardrobe.'

Tash sighs. 'I don't know, I've been here nearly three weeks and she don't go anywhere and she's got no friends. So if she has got a dealer she must be seeing them when I'm doing my day shifts.'

'Is that right?' Oobie shouts at me. 'You got someone helping you?'

'Oobie,' Tash says, throwing him a warning look. 'Keep your voice down 'cos the window's open.'

Oobie stares at me and I can see him churning over what Tash has just said.

'Well?' he demands. 'Who put the safe in for you? Your dealer?'

'Aaron put it in,' I say.

'Fuck me, Tash,' Oobie shouts. 'She's like a fucking parrot. How did you put up with her for all this time? I don't know why she thinks she can keep all the gear and the cash. I mean, what the fuck does she want it for? She's hardly going to go out and sell it.' Oobie sits himself down onto the bed and glares up at me.

'Come on Ellie,' Tash says soothingly. 'Just tell us the number, it'll be a lot easier if you just tell us.'

'I don't know it,' I repeat.

Oobie jumps up off the bed and stands over me before grabbing hold of my arms so tightly that I can't move.

'TELL ME THE NUMBER,' he shouts, inches from my face. spittle flying out of his mouth in rage. I recognise the signs and realise that he has the same hair-trigger temper that Aaron had. Oobie always seemed the quiet one when he used to sit in the lounge drinking lager and smoking joints with Aaron but perhaps he was afraid of Aaron as much as I was. I thought that Oobie was the only one of Aaron's mates who was normal because he actually had a job and didn't rely totally on thieving and dealing.

'I don't know it,' I repeat.

'Okay, don't say I didn't warn you,' he growls, his nails digging into the flesh on my arms and his face looming closer to mine. I stand immobile, refusing to flinch and he suddenly releases me so quickly that I nearly fall over. He bends down and picks up the holdall from the floor and throws it onto the bed and starts to unzip it.

'Close the door,' he barks at Tash over his shoulder. 'And shut the window 'cos we don't want the whole fucking street to hear.' He pulls a claw hammer out of the holdall and then reaches in and withdraws a screw driver that's been sharpened to a lethal looking point. Tash goes over to the chest of drawers and leans across over it and pulls the window shut and locks it and then tugs the flimsy curtains closed. I can still see daylight showing through them but people won't be able to see in even if they were looking, which they won't be. She turns and comes towards me and I know she's going to shut the door. I briefly consider making a break for it but realise that it's futile; I won't get very far with two of them after me. The front door is locked so I'd have to get down the hallway, unlock the door and do it all before they catch me.

Not possible; my legs have somehow turned to jelly and feel as if they can barely hold me upright let alone propel me out of the room.

'So, Ellie,' Oobie looms over me, the hammer in one hand and the screw driver in the other, a grim look on his face. 'It's your last chance, what's the number?'

He's going to torture me for the safe number and there's nothing I can do about it. I should just tell him the number now, of course, and make it easy on myself but I have a feeling that it's already too late because Oobie has that same glint in his eye that Aaron used to have; the one that meant he was enjoying himself.

It feels as if it's been going on forever and I wonder if it's ever going to end. Oobie's hair is plastered to his head with sweat and his face has turned a shade of deep, unflattering red. With the window and door closed the heat in the room is stifling and Oobie's rage is making him clumsy and the screw driver slips yet again. I'm sitting on the bed and Tash is next to me and I can feel that she's had enough.

'Just tell him the number, Ellie,' she whispers. 'Then we can stop all this.'

'I don't know it,' I say, for what feels like the hundredth time.

'I've done it! I've fucking done it!' Oobie suddenly shouts from the wardrobe.

He has indeed; the end of the screwdriver is now sticking out of the safe and Oobie has managed to lever open one corner of the door. If he can do the same on the other side he'll be able to pull it open.

'You could have made this a lot easier, you know,' Oobie glares at me. 'You'd better hope none of the stuff in there is damaged or else you'll be paying for it.'

I keep my face impassive and say nothing. Oobie seemed to think that because he was Aaron's friend he knew all of his secrets but he didn't; I don't have Aaron's stash or money but I know where it is; sort of – somewhere in the town an unsuspecting motorist is driving around with a wodge of cash and a big bag of pills hidden in their car that they have no idea about. Unless they've found them by now, which is always possible, but whatever's happened to them, Oobie won't be getting his hands on any of it. I so want to laugh but I don't because I don't think it'll end well for me if I do. I also think that if I start laughing I might not stop.

I could tell Oobie the truth about Aaron's stash and cash but he wouldn't believe me, because why would Aaron tell me about it when he wouldn't even tell his best mate?

Because Aaron didn't trust Oobie, obviously. He didn't trust me either but he couldn't resist showing off when he'd had a skin full. He also thought that I was so thick and afraid of him that there was no possibility of me telling anyone else.

Besides, who would I tell? I have no friends or family so his bragging was safe with me and to be fair, what he did *was* quite clever, especially as he wasn't that bright.

When Aaron did his dealing he didn't want to carry all the cash and his stash with him; it was too much of a risk if a club got raided and he was in there selling. To minimise the risk he only ever took in what he knew he'd sell so that if he had to he could drop it on the floor and kick it away into the corner. The place he used to hide it was simple and it was easy for him because he'd been stealing cars for years. Not new cars that were difficult to get into, worth lots of money and with fancy alarms, no, he'd steal old bangers that were easy to break into and jump start. He'd steal them late in the evening, so that often they weren't even reported missing until the next day. He'd drive them to a car park near where the clubs were and park in a dark spot at the back, somewhere out of sight. He'd hide his stash and drugs inside the car, either underneath the carpet in the front or underneath the front seat of the car if he couldn't get the carpet up. When his stock got low or he had cash to offload he'd slip out of the club and leave it in the car and then collect it all at the end of the night. It had never failed him, he said, and he'd been doing it for years. I must admit to being slightly impressed but it wouldn't have done for me, not that I'm a drug dealer, because there *was* an element of risk involved, despite him thinking he was so clever. Because what if someone had stolen the stolen car? You never know; it's unlikely but not impossible. I like to be sure of things and eliminate all risk.

There's a loud crack and I watch as the safe door swings open. Tash jumps up from the bed and dashes over to Oobie and kneels down on the floor next to him. I brace myself and wait for the inevitable.

'It's empty,' Oobie screeches, looking over at me with hatred. 'It's fucking empty.'

CHAPTER EIGHTEEN

'**W**here is it?' Oobie demands.

'Where's what?' I ask.

Oobie jumps up and launches himself at me and before I can move I find myself pinned flat on my back to the bed with Oobie on top of me.

'I'm fast losing fucking patience with you,' he growls into my face.

I suddenly want to go to the toilet when I realise that just because he didn't torture me for the safe number doesn't mean that he can't now. If he's anything like Aaron – and I'm sure he is – then nothing is out of bounds to get him what he wants.

'Oobie, stop,' Tash calls from behind him. 'Don't do something you'll regret.'

'I won't regret anything,' Oobie says, putting his hands around my throat. 'I'm going to enjoy strangling this stupid bitch.'

I feel his hands tighten and I can't breathe.

'Oobie.' I hear Tash shout from a long way away. 'Stop! 'cos how are we gonna get rid of a body?'

The room grows darker and darker and I stop struggling to breathe and my last thought as the world turns to black is that I'm so glad I found a new hiding place for my stuff because even though I won't live to enjoy it, at least they'll never get their hands on it.

I open my eyes and the room is in darkness, just the outline of the chest of drawers in the gloom confirming where I am. I wonder if I'm dead and am doomed to haunt this flat for eternity.

This notion is quickly dispelled by the agony of trying to breathe, my throat is so sore that just drawing in breath is excruciating. I can hear voices from the hallway and what sounds like things being thrown around. I slowly haul myself upwards and sit for several minutes trying to stop the dizziness and spinning in my head. I touch my fingers to my throat and wince; it's painful to touch and I guess that my throat is bruised black and blue by Oobie's hands. Tash must have stopped him from killing me – not because she's my friend but because getting rid of my body would be an inconvenience.

From the banging around and muffled curses I

think that they're ransacking the flat looking for Aaron's stash. I could tell them the truth about where it is but they won't believe me; they're convinced I've hidden it somewhere and they intend to find it. I need to think what I'm going to do because I think that Oobie is prepared to do anything to get his hands on that money.

The bedroom door flies open with a bang and Tash stands in the doorway looking at me.

'You alright, mate?' she asks, as if I've had a dose of the flu.

'No,' I croak.

'What are you like, eh?' She rolls her eyes and tuts. 'Why don't you just tell him where it is and then we'll leave you alone. It's not like you need the money for anything, is it? You don't go anywhere or do anything so you might as well give it up.'

I say nothing.

'You should 'fess up 'cos he's ripping your flat apart,' Tash says. 'There won't be nothing left of it by the time he's finished. He's going to start taking your sofa apart in a minute.'

I say nothing and Tash sighs and comes over to the bed and puts her arm around me and helps me to stand up.

'Come on, he wants to talk to you.'

I feel better standing up, more in control. I follow Tash out into the hall which is filled with the contents of the hall cupboard. My vacuum cleaner is on the floor and the bag has been ripped open and the contents scattered everywhere.

'See,' Tash say, noticing me looking at it. 'Look how much work you've made for yourself. You're going to have to clean all this up.'

She tuts and carries on through to the lounge and I follow behind her. The sofa has been pushed away from the wall and Oobie has the screwdriver in his hand.

'It's alive, then,' he sneers, looking at me.

'Tell him, Ellie,' Tash says. 'Cos your sofa's gonna be ruined if you don't.'

I stare at him dumbly and thank my lucky stars that I took all of the cash out and banked it.

'No?' Oobie questions, both hands gripping the handle of the screwdriver. I say nothing and watch as he pushes it into the material on the back of the sofa and pulls downwards. He then moves along to the other end and repeats the process before ripping the screwdriver along the top of the sofa. The material falls to the floor revealing the inside of the sofa.

He pulls his iPhone from his pocket, turns the torch on and shines it into the inside, crawling along the floor as he sweeps the beam into the sofa. Satisfied that there's nothing hidden there I watch as he repeats the process on the armchair and once that's done he scrambles around to the other armchair and starts to rip the back off.

'Tell him, Ellie,' Tash says. 'Cos it's the telly next and it's not going to work once he's finished with it.'

I don't care about the telly, or the sofa, or the flat,

but I do care about what he's going to do when he doesn't find anything because I don't fancy being opened up with that screwdriver.

'I don't know, honestly, I don't know nothing.' I croak, throwing in a double negative to make myself sound convincingly thick.

'You,' Oobie says, pointing the screwdriver at me, mid-tear. 'Are seriously pissing me off because I've got to go on shift in a minute and I wasted the whole fucking day here.'

'Sorry,' I whimper pathetically. 'I wish I could help.'

He glares at me before turning his head away and resuming his ripping and opens up the back of the chair. He clicks his torch on and shines it inside, and sweeps the beam of it around.

'Yes!' Oobie shouts suddenly in triumph. 'Yes! I fucking knew it!'

Tash and I watch as Oobie holds up a wad of notes in his hand; a wad of notes neatly bundled together with an elastic band.

Looks like I missed one.

He took the back of the telly off anyway; not content with finding over eight hundred pounds in the armchair, Oobie was convinced there was more. Tash made him unscrew it carefully and put the panel back on once he could see there was nothing in there because she said that living here would be beyond boring without a telly to watch.

What's going to happen is this; Tash is going to stay here with me because Oobie is convinced that I have an accomplice – he didn't use that word, far too big for him, he said *dealer* – and Tash is going to stay here until they find out who it is. This dealer has Aaron's stock and they want it back and Tash will watch me every minute of the day until they find out who it is.

Oobie says I could avoid all this if I just tell them who it is now and then Tash won't be staying here with me. If I tell him now, Tash will be staying here with Oobie and I'll be the one leaving. He says that he doesn't care where I go as long as he never has to look at my stupid face again. He says that as soon as they find out who I'm using to deal I'll be going anyway so I might as well make it easy on myself and tell him now.

I said I don't have a dealer and I'm pretty sure Oobie wanted to hit me then but Tash stopped him and said that he'd better calm down because she wasn't going to clear up his mess for him if he *lost it*. She said that she'll find out who it is but it just might take a bit of time. Thankfully, Oobie is not staying here because he can't stand to be around me. Tash has to sleep in the bed next to me so I don't sneak off – because whoever is dealing will eventually have to contact me – and then they'll catch them. I even have to go to work with her for her lunchtime shifts so that I'm not left here on my own.

So I'm going to be a prisoner in my own flat and there's no chance I can run away and start my new life. How I wish I'd gone when I had the chance instead of sticking around here because I didn't have the guts to do it. I wish I did have a dealer because then I could tell them who it is and I'd be free, but I haven't, so I'm stuck here forever or until Oobie decides he's had enough and kills me.

I've run out of options and I feel sad about that because I liked Tash, I really did, and things could have been so different but it is what it is, we have to play with the cards we're dealt.

It's obvious to me now that I'm going to have to kill again or else I'll have no life – and before you go thinking that I'm the sort of person who enjoys murdering people, I'm not; I only kill when I'm absolutely forced into it and have no choice.

And I have no choice.

Which will make me a serial killer if you count Mimi as number one. I Googled it after I killed Aaron and if you commit three murders it means that you're officially a serial killer – but if I don't count Mimi then I won't be because that would only be two murders.

Unless I kill them both, of course.

CHAPTER NINETEEN

It's all very well deciding to commit murder but in reality, it's going to be impossible. Tash is stuck to me like glue for twenty-four hours a day and the only place I'm able to go without her is the bathroom or the kitchen to make a cup of tea and if I take too long about that she checks on me. I can't even have a shit without her hammering on the door of the bathroom to ask what I'm doing.

How can I plan a murder with no phone, no money and no idea how I'm going to do it?

I can't.

I can't get to my hiding place to get my phone or money with Tash with me all of the time. I honestly don't know how I'm going to get out of this. I lay awake last night while Tash slept next to me and tried desperately to think of a way out but by the time dawn broke I was no nearer to a solution. It wasn't lost on me that I could have murdered Tash while she slept by putting a pillow over her face and suffocating her. It was tempting and it would have been easy. Or I could have strangled her with the lanyard that has the front door key on it that she wears around her neck and never takes off.

I can't even get out of my own flat.

Tash and Oobie must be very sure that I'm not going to fight back because Tash and I are a similar size so I could, in theory, over-power her. They have no idea that I murdered Aaron or what I'm capable of. Which should give me an advantage over them but it doesn't because even if I did suffocate her it would be pretty obvious that I'd done it and I'd end up going to prison. And then I would have achieved nothing, except for exchanging one prison for another.

I have considered just running; taking off in just the clothes I'm standing up in. Although I wouldn't be able to do this while Tash is sleeping next to me for two reasons; firstly, I'd have to climb over her to get out of the bed and as soon as I attempt any sort of movement she wakes up. Secondly, the key to the front door is on the lanyard around her neck; so even if I managed to get out of bed without her knowing, I'd never get the lanyard off without waking her up.

The only place I could make a run for it would be when we're at work in the chippy. I could pretend to go out into the back kitchen to go to the toilet and not come back.

But I don't think it would work; I have no money at all because my post office account is empty. I have lots of money in my secret accounts but to access it I need to get to my hiding place and it's right over the other side of town. How do I get there? I could get the bus but do I really want to wait around at the bus stop when I'm trying to make a run for it? I could take my chances and just run; run as fast and far as I can. But if I can run, so can Tash, plus Oobie has a car so I'd have no chance if he came after me. At best I'd only have a short head start before Tash noticed that I was missing.

It may come to that but not yet.

If I think about it long enough there must be a solution.

There is an easy way out of this; I could tell them about Mimi's money and give them some of it. I have given this serious thought and if I could just give them some of it and keep the rest for myself, I would definitely do it. The trouble is that to give them some of it I'd have to go and get my stuff from my hiding place and they'd insist on coming with me. Once they've seen how much I've really got, there's no way that they'd let me keep any of it; they'd take it all and I'd be left with nothing.

And then they'd probably kill me anyway.

Fred's a tight bastard; he hasn't even asked me why

I'm coming to work with Tash on her lunchtime shifts. She makes me stand behind the counter with her so that I can't get away and of course, I end up serving customers and taking their money but Fred never offers to pay me even though the shop is really busy. This is the third day that I've done it and I can tell that Tash is as fed up with it as I am. Oobie keeps ringing and pestering her and he comes into the chippy at least three times every afternoon and glares at me and calls me names when Fred's out of earshot. Luckily he's at work at night so he doesn't come to the flat but I'm dreading the weekend. He's going to be there all the time because he won't be working and he'll be starting on me again. I think it might be the last weekend that I'm alive because they've probably worked out how to dispose of my body by now.

Tash doesn't bother making any pretence of being my friend now; when we're at the flat we sit and watch television in silence or she's on her phone all night. The only time she speaks to me is to tell me what Oobie is going to do to me if I don't tell them who my dealer is. It doesn't make for pleasant listening and I can see that she enjoys the look of fear on my face as she becomes ever more graphic about the pain he's going to inflict on me. We have no food in the flat at all either except for some milk that Tash bought because she can't stand drinking black tea. We've been eating from the chip shop every day and if I never see another chip in my life it'll be too soon, although to be fair,

I hardly have an appetite as being shit-scared kills any desire for food.

And just when I think that things can't possibly get any worse, just after the lunchtime rush is over and we're clearing up, Stacey comes into the shop. I watch her as she comes in from the street and surprisingly, she looks okay, better than she ever looked when she was working here. Her hair is freshly washed and tied up into a neat pony-tail and she looks like she has a bit of makeup on. Instead of the usual skimpy tops she used to wear that barely restrained her tits, she has some sort of blue uniform on which actually suits her. My stomach flips when I see her because she's going to start on me because she blames me for Fred sacking her. I don't think I can take much more; I might as well just give up now and throw myself in the fryer.

I decide I'll go and stand in the back kitchen with Fred to get away from the nastiness and hope that she doesn't come around to the back entrance to get to me. I sidle towards the door but she spots me and I stand like a rabbit caught in the headlights. If I just stand here and let her have her say maybe she'll go.

'Hiya, Ellie,' she says, stepping up to the counter with a smile. 'How's it going?'

'Hello,' I manage to say after a moment, in total shock. 'Good, thanks. How are you?'

'Pretty good, ta. Got myself a new job, better than this dump.'

'Great,' I say, aware that Tash is staring daggers at me. 'I'm glad it's worked out for you.'

'Thanks,' Stacey says, studying my face. 'Maybe you should leave here too, 'cos Tash ain't the friend you think she is.'

I turn and look at Tash, who's leaning against the back wall with her arms crossed.

'Did you want something?' Tash says, uncrossing her arms and sauntering over to the counter. 'Or have you just come here to whine?'

'Just wanted to show you that you ain't won, you bitch,' Stacey says, with a scowl.

Tash smirks and doesn't move.

'You actually did me a favour,' Stacey says. 'Cos I've got a better job now with proper pay.'

'Good for you,' Tash says, sarcastically. 'Real career move eh, working in the station sweet shop.'

'Better than you and your druggy boyfriend can manage, though, eh? He's only fit for sweeping,' Stacey says.

'Fuck off,' Tash says, before quickly checking that Fred's not in earshot.

'Yeah, I'm going, but not 'cos you told me to. Think you're it, don't you, Tash? I never should have trusted you, 'cos you'll never change. You were a lying bitch before you got fucking locked up. But you're not as clever as you think you are and once those looks have gone all you'll have left is a record you can't hide and a skanky boyfriend.' Stacey turns and walks towards the door and pulls it open. She's about to go out when she turns and looks at me.

'Watch your back, Ellie, 'cos she's a sly cow. She tried to make out you set me up but I always knew it was her. No offence but I know you ain't got the brains to do something like that.'

And with that, she's gone.

'Stupid bitch,' Tash mutters and I look at her; I mean really look at her, and the seed of an idea to get myself out of this mess starts to germinate.

Maybe all is not lost, after all.

CHAPTER TWENTY

I t has to be tonight because today is Thursday which means the weekend, and Oobie, are only a day away. I wish that I'd thought of this plan sooner but there's nothing I can do about that now; I just have to get on with it and hope that it works. It would have been better to have more time to get things ready but it's still doable, if I'm careful.

We'll be going back to the flat after the lunchtime shift for a couple of hours before our shift starts tonight and I have to get everything ready then or it won't work. If I really can't do it tonight I might still be able to do it tomorrow, if I absolutely have to.

But I don't want to leave it until tomorrow because that will be my very last chance and if it doesn't work then I'm definitely going to be dead by the end of the weekend.

As I wrap fish and chips and take money from customers, my mind is working overtime. I can do it, I keep telling myself, I can do it if I hold my nerve.

I *have* to do it; I have no choice.

And if it goes wrong?

Then I'll end up going to prison or being murdered by Oobie. I want neither but if I have to choose I'll take prison.

If it works, I'll be free to start my new life.

As we walk home, Tash can't stop talking about Stacey and what a skank she is. She keeps telling me what a fuck-up Stacey was at school and all of the bad things that she did. I know now that Tash is lying; I can't trust one single word that comes out of her mouth and I wonder that I ever did. For some reason she's trying to convince me that Stacey is a liar and I don't know why, why does it matter what I think of Tash now? She's not my friend and never was; if I've re-learned one thing it's that I can't trust people. I never trusted anyone before I met Tash but she fooled me by being nice to me but that will never happen again.

Never, ever, again.

We arrive back at the flat and Tash opens the front door with the key and we go inside. Once inside she locks the door from the inside and tucks the key and lanyard back underneath her top. I go straight down the hall to the kitchen and put the kettle on. Tash follows me and lingers for a moment watching me before turning towards the lounge.

'I'm going to sit down,' she says as she goes. 'I need to put my feet up so bring my tea in.'

I don't answer but take two mugs down from the cupboard and fling a teabag into each and consider spitting into Tash's mug. It would give me a small amount of satisfaction but I don't because my mouth is so dry with nerves that my lips are stuck to my teeth so I have no saliva in my mouth at all.

I cross to the kitchen doorway and lean out and quickly check the hall to make sure that she's in the lounge. All clear; I hurry over to the corner wall cupboard and open the door. I take down a plastic sandwich box from the top shelf and open the lid as quietly as possible. Once opened, I pause for a moment and listen; I hear the murmur of the television and I guess that Tash has settled down on the sofa. I stare down at the jumble of Paracetamol packets, ibuprofen and plasters inside the sandwich box. Relief floods through me when I see the corner of the white cardboard box at the bottom of the box. I grab the box and quickly pull out a foil packet from inside and tuck them into the top of my jeans.

I replace the lid and put the plastic box back up on the cupboard shelf and quietly close the door. The kettle boils and I make the tea, splash some milk in and take the mugs through to the lounge.

I hand Tash her mug and she takes a slurp.

'Don't suppose we've got any biscuits?' she asks.

'No,' I say, sitting down in the armchair opposite her. 'I haven't got any money until I get paid tomorrow.' And I know I won't be allowed to keep it because she'll take it off me.

Tash tuts and carries on watching the television.

I drink my tea and when I've finished I stand up.

'Where are you going?' Tash demands.

'For a shit,' I say.

'There's no need to be so gross,' Tash says, pulling a face. 'Don't be long,' she calls as I leave the lounge.

As soon as I get into the bathroom I lock the door and lower the seat down on the toilet and sit on it. I pull the packet of sleeping tablets out of my pocket and pull off several sheets of toilet paper from the roll. I've never taken any of these tablets; when the social worker gave them to me after Mimi died I nearly threw them away but decided not to; how lucky was that? I don't know how many tablets I need to use and I can't even Google it because I don't have my phone. The recommended dose is one tablet so I decide four should do the trick. If four isn't enough I have tomorrow night for another attempt. I crush four while they're still in the packet and then carefully put my finger nail through the foil and tip the crushed tablets into the toilet paper. When all of the powder is sitting in the middle of the paper I carefully fold it over several times and twist it into a wrap. It's not ideal and I hope it doesn't tear. I poke the wrap of toilet paper into the corner of the window-sill behind the blind. The blind is permanently pulled down and Tash would have no reason to look behind it unless she's suspicious. I think that leaving it there is safer than carrying it around with me.

'What are you doing in there?' Tash shouts from outside the door.

I don't answer but flush the toilet and quietly lift the seat up and then open the bathroom door.

'What's taken you so long?' she asks, frowning. I didn't think I'd been very long but she's suspicious now.

I shrug and go to walk past her but she stops me and sniffs.

'I can't smell anything,' she says, narrowing her eyes.

I stare at her blankly.

'So what have you been doing in here?' she asks.

'You know what I've been trying to do,' I say. 'And I can't do it. Living on chips for a week has left me so bunged up that I can't even fart.'

'Yeuw,' Tash says, wrinkling her nose, as she turns to leave. 'Too much information.'

We walk down the hall to the lounge and I wish the hours away.

Not much longer now.

I lay in bed and listen to Tash breathing; it's steady and slow and she's been asleep for over an hour so I need to act now and stop dithering about. Five more minutes, I tell myself, I'll give her five more minutes to be absolutely sure and then I'll try and get the lanyard off from around her neck.

It was much easier to slip the sleeping tablets into her tea than I thought it would be – the hard bit was getting the powder to disappear so she wouldn't see it. I poured half a cup of boiling water onto the tea bag, chucked the powder in and then topped it up with more boiling water and milk and stirred and stirred and stirred. Whilst I was doing this she was flopped on the sofa moaning at what a hard night she'd had at the chippy. I was working right next to her but for some reason she thinks she's the only one who does anything. As soon as we got in I went straight to the bathroom and retrieved the twist of paper with the powder in and then went to the kitchen and made a cup of tea. When I took it in to her and put it on the table, I had to make myself look away to stop from watching her drink every mouthful of it. I was willing her to drink it and if she hadn't I don't know what I'd have done.

When we finally went to bed she fell asleep immediately – this isn't unusual as she normally does and she seems fast asleep so I need to get on with it.

Taking a deep breath, I sit up in bed and move around until I'm facing Tash. I can barely see what

I'm doing as it's so dark but my eyes gradually become accustomed to the gloom and I pull the duvet back and feel around her chest for the lanyard. When I find it, I grab hold of it and pull it upwards towards her head; she doesn't move or even stir. The difficult part is going to be getting it over her head. I put my hand underneath her head and attempt to raise it from the pillow. It's much harder than I thought it would be and I have to give up because her head's too heavy.

I decide that I have no choice but to go for it and I grab the lanyard firmly and haul it over her head and hair and drag it along the pillow. She makes a moaning noise as it catches her hair but she doesn't wake up. Lanyard and key in hand, I waste no time and carefully climb over her and pad silently across the room to the door, pausing only to pick up Tash's phone from the bedside table and a pair of trainers from the floor.

I tiptoe down the hall to the bathroom and once inside I close the door and put the light on. I quickly get dressed and put the lanyard around my neck. I take my watch from the bathroom shelf and strap it around my wrist; it's one-twenty-five.

I creep down the hallway, trainers in hand, and pause outside the bedroom and listen for a moment to the steady sound of Tash's breathing. Satisfied that she's still sleeping soundly I continue to the front door and unlock it. I let myself out into the communal corridor and lock the door and slip my feet into the trainers. I tie the laces tightly as they're slightly too big. I then zip up the hoodie and pull the hood over my head and down low so it's just above my eyes. I run silently down the three flights of stairs and into the communal hallway and slip through the double doors and out into the open air. A sliver of moon casts a dim light, it's just enough to see where I'm going as most of the street lights are out. I shiver, the night cooler now that we're into September; or maybe it's nerves. Thankfully, there's no one around to see me as I walk quickly across the grass and into the back alley that runs behind the chippy. This is a slightly longer route to get to my destination but far safer. I'm less likely to encounter traffic or people along the backs of the houses.

Once I'm in the safety of the dark alleyway I pause for a moment and stretch my arms up high over my head in an effort to release the tension from them. I take a deep, steadying breath in through my nostrils and blow it out slowly through my mouth.

I'm ready.

I jog slowly down the alleyway.

And then I break into a run.

CHAPTER TWENTY-ONE

Tash keeps on moaning; ever since we arrived at the chippy for her shift she hasn't stopped. How tired she is, what a rotten headache she has, how ill she feels, on and on and on.

I think even Fred's had enough of her and for once, she looks a bit rough. Normally fresh-faced and perky, even after staying up all night, today her eyes are puffy with dark circles underneath and her skin looks blotchy and uneven. It's obviously the effects of the sleeping tablets; maybe four tablets was a step too far. I suppose I'm lucky I didn't kill her.

'You going to stand there moaning all day or are you going to serve some bloody customers?' Fred demands, as he comes out from the kitchen with a fresh load of chips which he chucks into the fryer.

Tash pulls a face and doesn't move from her position of leaning against the back wall.

'I think I'm sickening for something,' Tash says. 'Ellie is coping alright.'

Yeah, Ellie who's not even getting paid for the shift. I take a five-pound note from another customer and ring it up on the till and give him his change.

'Go home, then,' Fred says.

'No, I'll stay,' Tash says. 'I'm supervising Ellie.'

Fred shrugs and wanders back into the kitchen; he's not going to argue when I'm working for free. I serve the next customer who takes his cod and chips and leaves and then the shop is empty. Tash sighs and pulls her phone out of her pocket and checks it for the millionth time today.

'Something wrong?' I ask.

Tash frowns and puts her phone back in her pocket.

'No.'

'You sure?' I ask. 'Cos you keep looking at your phone like you're expecting something.'

'Mind your own business,' Tash mutters.

The doorbell dings and a harassed looking woman with two screaming kids comes in and I walk over and begin to serve them.

Ten to two.

I don't think it can be very much longer.

And just as I have that thought, Tash's phone rings and she answers it. I serve the woman as quickly as I can, giving her a mammoth portion

NOT YOUR AVERAGE GIRL

of chips that she hasn't paid for in the process. I want her and her gobby brats out of the shop so that I can hear what Tash is saying. When the door finally closes on them I turn around to look at Tash and her face is a picture; I mean a real picture. Her skin has turned ashen which highlights the blobby bits even more and she looks dog-rough. Stacey's words about Tash's looks not lasting forever pop into my head. This is a glimpse of Tash's future and I enjoy the prospect of her turning into an overweight, aging tart who wears too much makeup.

'What's up?' I ask, as she slowly takes the phone from her ear.

The silence hangs for a moment before she answers.

'That was Oobie's brother,' Tash says.

'Oh, yeah?' I say. I didn't know he had a brother. I wonder if nastiness runs in the family.

'Yes,' Tash says robotically. 'There's been an accident.'

'Accident?' I echo. 'Oh, no, what's happened? Has Oobie been hurt?'

'No,' Tash shakes her head. 'He's dead.'

I honestly think that Fred expected me to stay and finish the shift and let Tash go home on her own. Tempting though that was, I felt it was my duty to come back with her to make sure she was okay.

Actually, I didn't have any choice about it because although Oobie is dead, nothing has changed. Tash still won't let me out of her sight.

I don't think Tash is heartbroken at Oobie's death even though he was her boyfriend. After the initial shock and the hysterical crying had subsided – personally, I think this was purely for Fred's benefit – Tash seemed more concerned about what she's going to do now, rather than the loss of Oobie. Unlike me, she's not a very good actress and I saw right through her. We'd hardly got back into the flat before she told me that just because Oobie's dead it doesn't mean that I'm free. She said that she has lots of friends far more frightening than Oobie so I needn't think for a minute that I'm going to get away with anything just because he's not around anymore. She says I'd better get my act together and 'fess up on who my dealer is or I'll be having an accident too.

I said nothing but went out into the kitchen to make a cup of tea; hot and sweet for her because she *has* had a shock, when all is said and done and also, she hates tea with sugar in it so why not? As the kettle was rattling through its boiling process I came to the conclusion that Tash is even more callous than me, and that's saying something. I made the tea and slopped three teaspoonfuls of sugar into hers and gave it a good stir and then took it through to the lounge and plonked it on the coffee table in front of her. She was on the phone to her mum and she'd turned on the heart-broken girlfriend act again.

'No, honestly, Mum,' she said between dramatic sobs. 'I'll be okay. I don't want to come home now, Ellie is looking after me but I'll be over to see you tomorrow.'

I couldn't hear what her mum was saying but it was in a soothing tone and she was sort of cooing. All the while her mum was talking, Tash was looking down at her nails and picking them and she wasn't even listening to her. When her mum finished, Tash ended the call and let out a big sigh before throwing her phone onto the sofa next to her. She stuck her bottom lip out and looked like a petulant kid.

'So what happened?' I ask, sitting myself down in the armchair opposite her.

'What?' She looks at me in confusion and I reprise my opinion of her being callous; I think she's an actual psychopath.

'Oobie's accident?' I prompt.

'Oh, that.' She picks up her phone again and begins scrolling. 'Something to do with falling onto a live line on the track, whatever that is. It was instant apparently. He wouldn't have suffered.'

'God, how awful.' I shudder. 'How did that happen? I thought he was just a cleaner, I didn't think they went anywhere near the railway.'

'He wasn't a cleaner,' she says, as if it matters. 'Just because that skank Stacey said it, she doesn't know nothing. He was a domestic associate and he worked all over the station. Wherever they needed him.'

A cleaner then.

'Okay,' I say, as if this explains everything.

We sit in silence and I drink my tea and Tash starts texting and before very long there's the ping, ping, ping of texts coming in on her phone. I guess that she's texted all her mates the sad news and they're all telling her how sorry they are. All the mates that I've never met.

'I think Fred should pay me whatsit money, you know, what they pay you when someone close to you has died,' Tash says.

'Compassionate leave?' I offer, forgetting that I'm supposed to be stupid.

'Yeah, that's it,' Tash says. 'I think I should get at least a week off on full pay, it's the least he can do.'

I'm trying to understand why Tash seems to think that it's somehow Fred's fault that Oobie has died when the doorbell shrills loudly. Tash and I look at each other in alarm because we never get visitors. Except for Oobie, and he's dead.

'Who's that?' asks Tash, as it shrills again.

'Only one way to find out,' I say, standing up.

They didn't want a cup of tea although I did offer to make them one and I was a bit surprised that they refused. Or maybe not; the flat looks so rough that they probably don't think they want to chance it. The sofa and armchairs have the backs hanging off where Oobie ripped them open so maybe they think that we live in squalor and don't wash the cups. I don't know; maybe they're just not thirsty.

There are two of them, which I expected, because they always send two to break bad news, don't they? Usually a man and a woman – at least that's what they do on the telly.

Oobie's brother had told them where Tash was living and as soon as she saw the uniform Tash burst into tears and put her heart-broken girlfriend act on again. The man is quite old, about forty, I'd say, and he's the one in charge because he's wearing normal clothes and not a uniform. The policewoman has a uniform on and she doesn't look any older than me. She looks fresh-faced and eager and I wonder at how different our lives are; I bet she never had a foster carer drag her up.

They've said how sorry they are but they haven't actually said what happened, just that Oobie is dead. And it turns out that Oobie wasn't his name at all, which I'd sort of guessed because who would give their kid a name like that? His real name was Owen Richards so who knows why he was called Oobie. It's a pretty stupid nickname if you ask me; not that it matters now.

'So, Miss Merrill, can you tell us when you last saw Mr Richards?' DI Prowley asks Tash.

Tash looks at him.

'I dunno, Monday, I think. We don't see each

other much during the week 'cos of our shifts. We work different hours, he does nights, see.'

He nods but doesn't scribble it in a notepad, like I thought he would, and nor does the policewoman.

'Why you asking?' Tash asks, with a hint of attitude, I think.

'With an unexplained death we have to ask these questions,' he says. 'It's procedure.'

'Unexplained?' Tash says. 'His brother said it was an accident. He said he fell on the tracks.'

'And where were you in the early hours of this morning?' he asks, ignoring what she's said. 'Can you tell us what you were doing at around two o'clock this morning?'

'What?' Tash jumps up from the sofa and I see that the waterworks are about to be turned on full blast again. 'Why are asking me these questions? Are you saying that it wasn't an accident? Did someone murder him?'

'I'm not saying anything, Miss Merrill,' he says. 'I'm simply asking you your whereabouts for the early hours of this morning.'

'Well, I was here, obviously, fast asleep like any normal person,' Tash shrieks. 'What a thing to ask when I've just lost the love of my life.'

'And do you have anyone who can verify that you were here all night?' he asks, completely unaffected by Tash's shrieking.

'Of course I do.' Tash looks at me. 'Tell him, Ellie, tell him where I was last night,' she demands.

I say nothing and look down at my lap and twist my hands together. There is a saying that revenge is a dish best served cold and as I sit here quietly, I savour the moment.

'Pardon?' I say, eventually, as if I haven't understood her.

'Last night,' Tash says impatiently. 'Tell them that I was here last night, sleeping next to you.'

I look down at my lap again.

'Yes,' I say, in a voice without emotion, slowly saying each word as if I've rehearsed them. 'Tash was here all night sleeping next to me.'

'There,' Tash says to DI Prowley. 'Now do you believe me?'

There's a moment's silence before DI Prowley speaks and he's speaking to me, not Tash.

'Is that true, Miss Sanders,' he asks gently, in a tone entirely different from the one he used with Tash. 'Did Tash spend the night here or did she tell you to say that?'

From his tone and the way he's speaking to me I know instantly that DI Prowley has already spoken to my social worker. He knows my name and obviously checked up on me and my history before he arrived here. I hear a gasp from Tash and I look up and see that she's opened her mouth to speak. DI Prowley holds up his hand to stop her.

'Please, Miss Richards, let Miss Sanders answer the question herself.'

I look up from my lap and stare at DI Prowley, trying to look as confused as possible.

'Um...'

He leans forward, his arms resting on his knees and looks at me earnestly. I stare at him with my mouth hanging open, probably the best thicko act that I've ever done. Really, I deserve an Oscar.

'There's nothing to be afraid of,' he says, gently. 'All you have to do is tell the truth.'

'She told me to say she was here,' I say, my words coming out in a rush.

'So she wasn't here, asleep in the bed next to you?' DI Prowley asks, gently.

'She's lying!' screams Tash. 'I was here all night, she's lying!'

'Quiet, Miss Richards,' he says calmly before nodding to the WPC who stands up and goes and stands behind Tash. I wonder if she's getting ready to snap the handcuffs on Tash's wrists if she attempts to make a run for it.

'Can you tell me what happened, Miss Sanders?' DI Prowley asks.

'She went out,' I say, my voice wobbling. 'And she left me for hours and hours and hours and I thought she'd never come back.'

'Please don't upset yourself, Miss Sanders, there's nothing to worry about. What made you think that she wouldn't come back? DI Prowley asks.

'Cos that's what she does,' I say. 'She says if I don't do as I'm told then she'll leave me.' I start to cry properly then, big heaving sobs that are even more dramatic than Tash's. I feel a trickle of snot escape one nostril but I deliberately don't wipe it away. DI Prowley watches me as I slowly hold up my arms and pull my sleeves down to reveal raw, bloody, rope marks around my wrists.

'She locks me in and ties me to the bed,' I say, between shuddering sobs. 'She says if I'm bad she won't come back and no one will ever find me and I'll die.'

DI Prowley stares at me and I can see that he absolutely believes me. It was very painful and time-consuming rubbing the nylon cord around my wrists until they bled this morning.

But so very worth it.

Out of the corner of my eye I see the WPC cover her mouth with her hand in shock.

'Sorry,' I say, in a pathetic tone, turning to look at Tash.

For once, she's lost for words and stares back at me in complete disbelief.

Gotcha.

CHAPTER TWENTY-TWO

As it turned out, I didn't have to lie very much to the police.

Apart from the one, enormous lie, of course.

I told them how Tash and Oobie had kept me prisoner to try to get me to tell them where Aaron's money was even though I knew nothing about it. I told them of my fear that Oobie was going to kill me if I didn't come up with the money by the weekend. I pointed out the ripped apart sofas and the prised open safe; Tash never stood a chance of them believing her because the evidence against her was overwhelming.

They totally believed everything that I said; not least because most of it was true and the evidence backed me up. They questioned Fred and when he confirmed that I'd started going into work with Tash every lunch time but I wasn't actually paid for the shift, that further sealed her fate. It didn't make Fred look very good either, because he looked like a tight-wad who took advantage of people with learning difficulties. Hopefully Social Services will pay him a visit in the not too distant future.

I told them that Tash had taken my purse away from me and that my Post Office account was empty. I had no money to buy any food and was totally reliant on Tash for everything. I said that Tash and Oobie has been starving me and I'd been reduced to stealing food from the chippy to eat – and that wasn't a lie, either.

When forensics searched the flat the results backed me up; there was no food in the cupboards and I had lost weight and it showed. I said the safe was Aaron's and I pretended that I knew nothing about his drug-dealing; a small lie which I made up for by telling them the truth of how he used to beat me and wouldn't leave when I asked him to.

They were very kind to me, the police; kinder than anyone has ever been to me in my life and I have to admit that I lapped it up. It was quite strange really because the kinder they were, the thicker I seemed to behave which made me even more of an obvious victim, and helped in their case against Tash.

DI Prowley in particular made a special effort with me and went above and beyond the call of duty. If he thought the questioning was getting too much for me he'd let me have a break and would send someone off to get me a sandwich and a cup of tea. I'd sit in the relative's room and eat it and stay there until I felt up to talking again. It would have been better if they'd had a telly in there because it got a bit boring but you can't have everything, I suppose. I'll miss that kindness when I start my new life but I won't miss having to be stupid all of the time because it becomes a bit tedious after a while.

Once my statement was complete they said that I'd only have to appear in court as a witness if Tash pleaded not guilty. I knew that there was no way Tash would plead guilty so I'll have to hang around for a bit longer before I can start my new life, which is a bit of a bummer. Once Tash is safely behind bars I'll be moving out of this horrible flat and finding myself somewhere much nicer to live, far, far away.

When they eventually charged Tash, it was with false imprisonment, threatening behaviour and actual bodily harm against me. The actual bodily harm charge was for tying me to the bed every time she went out.

And I said she'd slapped me around a few times as well.

But the main charge, of course, was murder.

Because apart from my statement that she wasn't with me that night, all of the evidence pointed to her pushing Oobie onto to the live track where he was electrocuted. Even without my statement they had her bang to rights, as they say. My witness statement was the icing on the cake and it wasn't actually necessary but I did it because as I've said before; I like to be sure of things. I can't be doing with any lose ends or element of doubt.

I know that Oobie's wasn't a quick death so the police aren't being truthful about that. I didn't hang around to watch but let's just say what I saw wasn't very pleasant. I only took a quick glance down onto the tracks to make sure that he couldn't get back up and I had to look away. I *almost* felt sorry for him until I remembered what he would do to me if he lived. The police said that his death was instantaneous – I think they only say this to save the family's feelings but I'm not sure if anyone really believes it. Tash doesn't care anyway because I don't think she has any feelings for anyone else; all she ever thinks about is herself and how everything affects her. I truly believe that she is a psychopath.

I do wonder if I might be a psychopath and I've given it a lot of thought and to be honest, I'm not sure. I think that realistically, how I conduct myself in the future will answer that question. And like I said before, technically I could already be classed as a serial killer if you include Mimi in the mix.

But for now; the jury's still out, as they say, on me.

The police had very grainy, black and white CCTV from the railway station showing Tash following Oobie along the platform when he went for one of his many illegal cigarette breaks. They also had shots of her coming into the station and jumping over the barriers instead of buying a ticket. Her features are fuzzy and of course her hood was up but there's no denying it was her because the clothes she was wearing were the same ones found in the laundry basket in the bathroom.

Oobie spent a lot of time in the remote area of the platform where he was out of sight of the cameras according to his work mates. It was his favourite skive area and reading between the lines of what I overheard at the police station, it was only a matter of time before he got fired as he was no model employee.

There was no actual footage of Tash pushing him but she was the only one that came back from his final cigarette break which just shows that smoking is a killer. Even without the CCTV footage fibres from Oobie's clothing were found on the sleeves of her hoodie; almost as if she'd pulled the sleeves over her hands before she pushed him.

The mobile phone records further sealed her fate by pinpointing her at the station at the time of Oobie's death, and there was no getting out of that one.

Tash protested her innocence, loudly and often, and told the police that I'd set her up, as I knew she would. I wasn't there when she made these allegations but from the snippets of conversation that I overheard between DI Prowley and his officers, it's clear that her claim was met with derision and disbelief. How could I, a girl with obvious learning and emotional difficulties, engineer such a thing? I was so gullible that I'd been targeted not once, but twice by manipulative dealers eager to use me and my flat for cover.

That's the thing with the thicko act; people sort of forget you're there and talk quite freely and say things to each other that they shouldn't. They think that you can't hear or understand them, you know, like when there's a dog or a cat in the room.

Yes, the police all agreed, it was implausible and laughable that I, a twenty-one year-old who worked in a chippy, would have the brains to frame Tash. That I could drug Tash so that she wouldn't wake up and then dress in her clothes, take her mobile phone and sneak into the railway station and murder her boyfriend.

Totally ridiculous.

And anyway, why? Why would I do it?

It makes no sense at all.

No. Tash just looked more and more desperate by trying to put the blame onto me. The more she protested that it wasn't her, the more convinced the police became that she was guilty. And her record didn't help either; all of those things that she told me about Stacey weren't true – it was Tash who went to youth custody for 'bottling' someone. She'd also been prosecuted so many times for shop lifting that she was lucky to even get a job in the chippy. I still wonder how she managed to convince Fred that it was Stacey who was stealing from the till when it was obviously her.

But I believed everything she said, didn't I?

Yes I did. And I think it's because she's so pretty; beautiful people get an easy ride through life, don't they? We like to believe everything that comes out of their mouths, especially when they're being nice about it. I think that the brain is somehow wired to believe that beautiful people are good and ugly people are bad; not fair at all, but that's how it seems to me.

Somehow, it's much easier to think someone is bad if they're ugly –the baddies in the fairy tales that we're brought up on are nearly always ugly women so I think it's preconditioned from childhood.

So there it is; the confessions of a serial killer – or a nearly serial killer.

Take your pick.

CHAPTER TWENTY-THREE

The September sun is shining through the clouds as I walk into the churchyard and I breathe in a lungful of fresh air and think how good it is to be alive, which is an odd thought to have in a place of the dead.

The last year has seemed never-ending at times. After the initial excitement of Tash's arrest and giving my statement to the police, the wait for the trial seemed never-ending. The wheels of British justice grind exceedingly slowly, even though DI Prowley told me that Tash's case went to trial extremely quickly.

It didn't feel quick to me at all but that doesn't matter now, because it's over and done with and Tash has gone to prison for a long, long time. She received a life sentence – which is fifteen years minimum. That's not really life, is it? Not unless you have a very short life.

Tash will still be a young woman by the time she's released, only thirty-six by my reckoning, so I think she's got off quite lightly. I wonder if she'll decide that she wants revenge on me for setting her up? If I was her I think that I definitely would but I have no fear that she'll find me. I'll be far, far away with a different name and a different life long before she hits the streets again.

By the time I was called to give evidence I was sick to death of pretending to be stupid but I consoled myself with the fact that it would be a part I'd have to play for the very last time. I gave it my best Oscar worthy performance and the jury were obviously convinced because they were unanimous in their verdict of *guilty* and took barely thirty-minutes to reach that conclusion.

Tash is in the process of appealing, of course, but it's pointless and a complete waste of tax-payers money. I don't think that it should be allowed when the evidence is so compelling. She'd do far better to resign herself to serving out her sentence and just getting on with it; maybe get herself an education or something.

She seems to have this fanciful idea that just because she's actually innocent of murder she'll be able to prove it.

The sun scuds behind a large cloud and the sky darkens and I can't help smiling to myself as I approach the graveside. It's all worked out unbelievably well, aside from the long wait.

I open the large carrier bag that I've brought with me and take out the bunch of flowers that I bought from the local Tesco's. I remove the cellophane wrapping and lay them on the top of the grave whilst I kneel down and remove the dead flowers from the urn. I come here every week to lay flowers at Mimi's grave and though I say it myself, it's one of the best looked after plots in the graveyard. I pick up the urn and twist around and empty the fetid, brown water onto the grass behind me. I pull the large plastic juice bottle from the carrier bag and unscrew the top. I filled it with water from the tap before I left home and it was heavy to carry but there is no tap here. Maybe the church should think about putting one in. As I tip the contents of the bottle into the urn I reflect that this will be the very last time that I visit Mimi's grave.

Glancing around the graveyard to make sure that I'm alone, I reach into the carrier bag and pull out a small metal trowel and force the pointed end of it into the ground in front of Mimi's headstone. The earth is hard where the urn protects it from the rain and I have to force it into the earth. Once it's nearly in I put both hands on the trowel handle and press down, flipping the hardened earth upwards. I grasp hold of the clump of earth and with a combination of pulling the clod and pushing the trowel I eventually lever it out of the ground. I turn the lump of earth upside down in my hand and study it and then pull out the tiny plastic bag which is embedded in the dirt. I rub off the excess mud and drop the plastic bag into the carrier bag. I then replace the clump of earth back into the hole and press down firmly with my hands and put the urn on top. I slot the flowers into the holes in the urn and admire my handiwork; that will do.

I put the trowel back into the carrier bag with the empty bottle and, keeping both hands inside the carrier bag, I rip open the tiny plastic bag that was hidden underneath the earth and remove the key. Using a wet wipe from the packet that I've brought with me, I carefully wipe the key clean and then tuck it into my pocket. I pull out several more wet wipes and thoroughly clean my hands before dropping the dirty wipes into the bag.

I stand up and dust off my knees, pick up the carrier bag and make my way towards the churchyard exit. As I pass the church I deposit the carrier bag and contents into the waste bin that's attached to the wall.

Visiting Mimi's grave has served its purpose and I reflect on the fact that Mimi was far more useful in death than she ever was alive.

How fortunate that I moved my money and cards when I did; if I'd delayed any longer then Tash and Oobie would have had everything and I would most likely be dead.

I've been very patient and waited until now to access my accounts so that there was no possibility that the police would discover the amount of money that I have. They had no reason at all to look, but as I've said before, I take no chances.

Until Tash was convicted and safely behind bars, I continued my dull and boring life. I even stayed working at the chippy and took over Tash's lunchtime shifts.

But I'm safe now; the furore over Tash has died down and the police no longer bother with me. The social worker is satisfied that I'm in steady employment and I've promised her that I'll contact her should anyone attempt to befriend me. She has other, more needy cases than I.

This afternoon I'll be collecting my stuff from the safety deposit box where it's been for over a year. It's much more secure than a safe in my bedroom and the majority of the banks offer this service now. I made sure to buy the premium package and have paid for five years in advance; slight over kill perhaps but I like to err on the side of caution. Aside from my purse and mobile phone, there is also a sizable chunk of cash to use for immediate living expenses. The mobile phone of course, will be completely flat, but once it's charged and I have everything that I need from it, I may treat myself to a new one. The latest model, most likely.

The only thing that you need to access a safety deposit box is a key. No photographic identification is required because the bank has my photograph on record and also my fingerprint. I made sure to choose one of the new, modern banks rather than one of the old fuddy-duddy ones.

The key problem caused me concern for a while; if Tash or Oobie were to find it and discover what it was, they would take if off me. Whilst they wouldn't have been able to get the box open without me, I didn't care for the thought of being taken at knifepoint to open it for them.

And then it came to me; visiting the graveside of someone who was practically a mother to me wouldn't be suspicious at all, would it? I didn't actually *need* to come every week; I came by choice so that I could make sure that no one else was visiting her grave.

The sun comes out from behind the cloud and the day lights up and I think, again, how very good it is to be alive.

Hello, new life, the sun seems to be saying to me.

It's time to be someone else.

Goodbye Ellie.

THE END

Thank you so much for reading this book, I really do appreciate it. I do hope that you've enjoyed it and if you have, please leave a review or star rating on Amazon/and or Goodreads.

Printed in Great Britain
by Amazon